# THE DRAGON'S COMPLIANT SACRIFICE

## THE LAST DRAGONS BOOK 5

INES JOHNSON

Edited by Enchanted Quill Press
Cover design by Jacqueline Sweet Designs

CHAPTER ONE

The smell of alcohol burned Elek's nostrils. As the only dragon in his weyr with cooking skills that went beyond skinning a kill and gobbling it down whole, he'd often put spirits in the pots and pans of the foods he prepared for his family. However, he'd never once drunk any of the liquid straight from the bottle, nor from the crystal goblets that the women in the castle insisted on, though he did covet the personalized charms the girls placed around their glass stems to identify which drink belonged to whom.

Cardi's charm was a silver fox with diamonds for eyes, in honor of her mate Kimber, Elek's eldest brother and de facto leader of their weyr. Chryssie, who'd mated Kimber's younger twin Corun, had a charm that was an angel with wings and the ruby-red fangs of a vampire. Chryssie had once told Elek it had something or other to do with a buff vampire slayer.

Poppy, his brother Beryl's mate, had an emerald owl for a charm, though she only imbibed fruit juices these days as her belly swelled with the next generation of dragons. Rose, the newest female in the dragons' castle, had yet to receive a charm. Though Elek knew his brother Ilia was fashioning his woman a flower made of jade.

Elek picked up the charmless glass and peered down. The liquid in the cup's belly had come straight from an old, dusty bottle off the top of the shelf of God's Teet. The Teet was the one and only watering hole in the Veil; that crack in the fabric of the earth where the Goddess had originally crafted Her treasured species.

Dragons had once been a favorite of Hers—until she'd begun tinkering with apes. The toddling primates had remained Her favorite to this day as they poked holes in the sky, dumped their refuse in the waters, and generally made a mess wherever they went.

A few dust particles drifted up and into the air. One dust bunny slipped past Elek's lips and dissolved on his tongue. It didn't take away from the burning scent of the alcohol.

The barmaid Mari hadn't bothered to remove any of the dust particles when she'd popped the cork and filled his glass. Elek saw a few unsanitary bits floating around on the surface of his drink. Wasn't it said that any object should sink once it was submerged in alcohol?

"Bottoms up," said Mari.

With one hand, the fairy shoved the mug into Elek's clenched fists, forcing his fingers open to receive the libation. At the same time, Mari downed a mug of her own, tipping the cup until all Elek could see was the bottom of the glass—and a few more unsanitary bits of flotsam and jetsam.

Elek wasn't a competitive dragon by nature, but when he saw the relief cross Mari's features after she'd downed the alcohol, he wanted that feeling for himself. He brought the mug to his lips and tipped it back—only to splutter, cough, and choke the moment the fiery liquid hit the back of his throat.

"Easy there, big guy. It's your first time."

This wasn't Elek's first time at God's Teet. He'd had a chaste fruit drink whenever he'd come in, flanked by his brothers. Fairies would approach him for amorous entertainments. He'd always wave them away, not interested in sullying himself with their flowery scents. He couldn't anyway. The beast within him would easily break their flexible limbs if it got its claws on them.

"Just take it slow this time," Mari was saying as she poured another drink for herself.

This certainly was a day of firsts for Elek. Other than Mari, no one had offered him the option to go slow. No one had even offered him the option to say no.

Which Elek had said.

Numerous times.

Unfortunately, his wishes didn't rank high on this particular matter.

Elek raised the mug to his mouth again. He heeded Mari's warning of going slow this time when he swallowed. The liquid was smoother as it went down his throat the second time, though it still burned.

Inside his gut, Elek felt the dragon stir. He used the meditation techniques that had been his constant for over half his life. He took in full deep breaths, letting the air seep slowly out of him. It was the best way to keep his volatile dragon under the staunchest of control. He had to. He couldn't have a repeat of his shameful past.

"Here's to shedding past mistakes," said Mari.

Elek lifted his head. Then had to immediately close his eyes. The vision of Mari standing behind the bar multiplied into two. Then back to one. Then to three.

Just two swallows of alcohol and he was already losing control. Just like he'd done back when he'd been a raging fledgling. He knew that alcohol hadn't been to blame back then. It had been the monster crawling under his flesh.

"You can't shed your mistakes," Elek said. "They stay with you. All you can do is accept what you've done and try to make amends."

"I didn't do anything wrong," said Mari, her words slurring as she poured her third cup of spirits. "I'm not the one that's gone and mated with a human after marking me."

"Marked you?" Elek gave his head a shake. "I never marked you."

He must have heard the fairy wrong. Dragons couldn't mark fairies. The two species were entirely incompatible. At least where it mattered.

Dragons and fairies could engage in coitus. In fact, the two breeds engaged in copious amounts of coitus. Sometimes out back of the bar.

However, by design, dragons and fairies couldn't

produce any offspring. Which was the purpose She had made all of Her creations for. The Goddess had made both male and female fairies. She had neglected to make dragon females.

Luckily, human women could bear whelps. Unluckily, the Veil that separated the human realm from the dragon realm was closed until further notice. Thanks to a dragon that had dared fall in love with one of Her daughters.

"I haven't even marked Lily yet," Elek continued. "That's what the liquid courage is for."

Elek raised the mug. The liquid inside sloshed over the rim.

Mari's eyes went wide as snowballs. She let out a long sigh that was tinged with a cold front. "You're the one that claimed the human? Not…."

In her pause, Elek understood Mari's unspoken meaning. "Lily is mine. Not his."

The relief in Mari's icy features was instant, as though the sun had come up over the winter fairy's head. But her secret childhood love with Rhyol was another story. Elek had his own drama to deal with.

No, he hadn't claimed Lily yet. He hadn't even marked her. He didn't trust himself to let out only his fangs in her presence.

What if it happened again?

What if the animal trapped inside him took another woman's life from her?

Elek knew this had to be done. The other shifters would fight to claim Lily if she was unmarked, unmated. She was far too fragile for that.

Elek had seen enough evidence of her fragility during the handful of days he'd known her. Lily was quiet, timid. She would retreat into herself if too many people were around, much like Elek was prone to do when it got crowded.

Lily loved to eat. Elek was happy to feed her. He delighted in watching her eat his food—she would close her eyes in ecstasy with each bite he prepared for her and….

Something below his belly button tightened at the memory of that. It was the beast stirring in its cage. Elek took a deep cleansing breath, focusing on calm and peace and nothingness until the dragon's roars in his mind were doused. But he knew it was only a temporary fix.

To save Lily and keep her safe, he'd have to let the beast out.

# CHAPTER TWO

There was a witch on Lily's back.

She felt the witch's claws pricking her spine. She knew that most adults had about twenty-four vertebrae along their spine. She swore she felt the witch digging her sharp nails into each one of hers. Maybe the hag was using her toes? Or maybe there was more than one of the creatures. Either way, there was nothing Lily could do about it.

She lay flat on her back, immobile on the soft mattress. Her eyes were open in the darkened room. The shadows moved across the walls, along the floors. They dipped and dived, edging closer and closer to her.

Lily couldn't scream. She couldn't call out for help. She couldn't lift a single finger to defend herself. She was awake, but trapped inside a nightmare as the hag held her down. She could do nothing but wait for the demons to release her.

Ever since she was a child, Lily had experienced these bouts of sleep paralysis. Each time, there was a heavy weight on her chest, making it impossible to rise, impossible to call out for help. She couldn't so much as wiggle her toes or even blink. She was a helpless captive.

The paralysis happened because the body was awake, but the brain was still shifting from REM sleep. Lily had learned that term as a teen. Being an insomniac, REM sleep was something she coveted. The downside of falling into the deep sleep of REM for someone like her—who routinely didn't get enough sleep—was the paralysis.

In REM sleep, the brain largely paralyzed the rest of the body so the person didn't try to act out their dreams. Lily's new friend, Chryssie, had said she often dreamed she was Buffy the Vampire Slayer, meting out justice to the undead villains of the world. Cardi imagined she was an 80's pop star in a sparkly tulle skirt, dancing on a raised platform in a shopping mall.

If their bodies allowed either woman to act out those dreams, they would hurt themselves. Or, at least, annoy their mates who slept next to them each night. So, the body turned off most motor function during deep sleep as a defense mechanism.

Only, it backfired on Lily.

As a child, Lily had heard the phenomenon described as *having a witch, or a hag, on your back.* As a child, she'd believed it, literally. She'd imagined a green witch with boils on her cheeks and a hooked nose, dressed in all-black—like the Wicked Witch from Oz. And because Lily had always been a fashionista, she'd imagined the witch wore black-and-white striped socks with the most gorgeous pair of ruby-red shoes.

Lily had always preferred Elphaba's dark fashions to Glenda's white princess get up. White was a tricky color to pull off, but black hid so much. And for so much of Lily's life, she'd had to hide so many of her imperfections.

Elphaba had had it right with her dark clothes and hat, with only her shoes as the pop of color. Lily and the witch would've been friends with that kind of fashion sense. Except for the whole making-Lily-an-immobile-prisoner-inside-her-own-body thing.

She knew there was no fashionable witch on her back. She knew there were no such things as witches. Or at least she didn't think there were?

Now that she knew dragons were real—as well as lions, and bears, and wolves, and even fairies—Lily didn't doubt that a witch could have landed on her back and sat there to keep her still and immobile and afraid.

"Lily. Wake up."

That wasn't a witch speaking to her now. Dark turned to a light brighter than the sun. More than anything, Lily ached to shut her eyes to the sudden brilliance.

The shadows fled into the corners and out the window as the light rushed into the room. A dark figure moved inside and came towards Lily. The figure was dark only because she was dressed in a jade-colored robe.

"Lily?"

A face that mirrored Lily's own peered down at her—her sister, Rose. More than anything, Lily wanted to wake up to Rose's voice. But the imaginary witch held her firm.

"Lily!"

Rose shook her hard. It was her touch that broke the witch's spell. Finally freed from the nightmare, Lily's limbs went into overdrive. She scrambled back to the headboard, her arms and legs flailing, her fingers and toes flexing and curling.

She panted as though she had just finished a marathon run.

"It's okay," said Rose, wrapping Lily up in her arms and squeezing tight. "I'm here. It's okay."

Lily buried her head in her sister's chest. Though they were twins, Rose's chest was a cup-size smaller —something talent agents and fashion designers had always remarked on, to Rose's ire.

But her sister's chest had always been a haven for Lily. The sound of Rose's heartbeat. The strength of her spindly arms. The certainty in her husky voice.

"It's okay. You're safe."

That definitely wasn't true. It had never been true a day in their lives. But Lily always appreciated the sentiment.

Rose and Lily had been pimped out since before they could walk. Pimped in the way that child performers were paraded in front of agents, photographers, and directors. Twins had always been a hot commodity in the performing arts. Twins with the good looks of the Bishop girls had brought money into the household from the day they were born. It had also brought the predators.

The Bishop girls might have looked like easy prey with their pixie-like bodies. Truth be told, Lily was easy pickings. But Rose had always been her champion. And now, Lily had six dragon-sized champions who would decapitate and burn to a crisp any male who dared to lay a hand on her.

So, for the first time in her life, it was true. Yet still, the witches came for her.

"Thanks," Lily said when her sister loosened her hold.

Lily didn't bother to ask how Rose had known she'd been in distress—they were twins. They often got a sensation when one needed the other. Here, lately, it was always Lily that needed Rose.

Out of the corner of her eye, Lily saw a figure in the doorway. Ilia stood sentry outside the bedroom. His gaze mainly stayed on Rose, but he slid a glance to Lily as well.

Lily knew that Ilia would risk his life for her just the same as he would for Rose. He'd proven that when Rose had insisted he mate Lily instead of her. The rules of this world were such that any unmated human woman was fair game to the male shifters who roamed the land. Ilia had fallen hard for Rose, but Rose loved her sister above anyone else.

Luckily for them, Ilia's brother Elek proved that he loved his brother too. Elek had agreed to mate Lily. Though she hadn't seen him since he'd made the claim.

"I'm okay now," Lily said. "You two can go back to bed. Or to whatever you were doing."

Lily looked down to see that Rose had a piece of twine tied around her wrist. The knot looked intricate, like a flowering rose. But the edges looked broken, as though it had been yanked free by a powerful dragon's hands.

"I'll stay with you," said Rose.

"No, I'm up now. I'm just going to go and get some food."

"It's late at night."

"Are you fat-shaming me?"

It was a joke between the two rail-thin women. Before coming to the Veil, Lily and Rose had suffered from a condition that turned their stomachs into knots. Nobody in the modeling world cared that the girls were malnourished and starving at the hands of the disease. They had been getting paid, but they were not living healthy, fulfilling lives.

That was a thing of the past. Here in the Veil, they could eat without restrictions. They could live without being bound to a scale. They could wear white anytime because there was no Labor Day here.

Their disease was a thing of the past. There was always plenty of food on the table. And no one to cast them a sidelong glance if they packed on the pounds.

Lily did cast a sidelong glance of longing as her sister and her mate left the room. Lily's belly was full, but there was still a hunger inside of her that was unsatisfied. Ignoring that sensation, she slipped into baggy pants and headed down to the kitchens in search of a meal.

CHAPTER THREE

Elek filled the measuring cup with flour. The white powder sifted into the mixing bowl, particle by particle. Much like the sands of his meditation hourglass. For more than half his life, Elek had spent many hours watching grains of sand fall through the curvature of the chalice. Watching as the buxom top half sent its calming treasures through a hungry channel and down into the—

"You realize you're going to have to plow her?"

The cup in Elek's hand shook. The flower spilled all over the counter in a plume of white. It reached his nose, tickling his nostrils. Elek held his breath, refusing to let the sneeze escape his body. He felt the dragon watching from its place in his belly.

"Corun did have the talk about the birds and the

bees with you, right?" Beryl went on, dipping his blunt finger into the discarded mixing bowl Elek had used to mix cookie batter.

"Birds and bees do not mate," said Corun. "I had the same talk with Elek as I had with you about the mechanics and biology of sexual intercourse."

"That's probably why he hasn't engaged in any." Beryl tossed the bowl into the sink. The glass container gleamed spotlessly as though it had been through the dishwasher and not licked clean by an overgrown dragon.

Elek remeasured a cup of flour and poured it into another bowl, quickly this time. He didn't allow the grains to sift slowly.

The recipe called for a pinch of salt, which made Elek's nose twitch. Not from the salt. Salt was a necessary seasoning in baked goods. Even in sweet treats, salt's job was to enhance the flavor.

What made Elek twitch was the use of a *pinch* as a measurement. Baking was a precise science. The pinch of *his* fingers was different from Beryl's big bear-claws, which would've rendered the sweet treat inedible.

Elek had made this same recipe with Lily a few nights ago. The pinch of her two slender fingers together was far too little, but Elek hadn't added more. His instincts had told him that Lily's addition would be the perfect amount—and he'd been right. The treat had been so delectable that he had elected not to share it with any of his family. He'd kept the pastries just between the two of them.

"It doesn't matter how he received his sex education," said Kimber, his large body leaned against the pantry threshold. His gaze was trained on Elek. "You must do this. It is your duty. Or there will be consequences."

Elek reached around his brother for a baking dish. He made quick work of buttering the pan before pouring in the batter. He took a deep breath, inhaling all the way down into his belly. As he exhaled, he loosened the reins of his beast—only a fraction.

A controlled stream of orange flame passed his lips which he aimed into the hearth. The wood caught the fire and began a slow burn. With the flame lit, Elek clenched his gut, locking his beast back into place.

He placed the baking pan directly on the flame and stepped back, admiring the glow. There had been a time when he'd wanted a gas stove with burners that he could control. But he now had complete control of the fire inside him.

"Elek, are you listening?" asked one of his brothers. "You can't ignore us."

Whichever of his brothers made that edict—likely Kimber—was wrong. Elek was excellent at ignoring the wayward thoughts in his mind. Meditation afforded him a perfect peace and escapism. He'd always been able to tune out—

"Something smells amazing."

At the sound of that buttery-soft, vanilla-sweet feminine voice, the air left Elek's lungs. In that breathless moment, his dragon reared its head. Elek turned and took in Lily with amber-bright eyes.

She stood in the doorway. Her body was covered in thick cloth. The fabric was the color of ripe peaches. Not an inch of skin was shown—unlike her sister, who preferred to prance around in as little clothing as possible. Still looking at her, Elek's mouth watered.

No. The dragon's mouth watered. Because the beast had slipped its leash.

Elek shut his eyes, taking in a deep breath. He filled his lungs until he felt himself about to burst. That only fueled the fire-breathing beast.

Quickly, Elek let out the air, evacuating all of the necessary ingredient that would give the dragon breath. Without any air, the dragon finally retreated, leaving Elek holding his breath.

"I'm sorry," Lily said into the silence. "I didn't realize you were all…. I'll come back."

"No!" Beryl, Corun and Kimber all called out in unison. Their collective voices caused the woman to jump. Elek wanted to put himself between her and his brothers.

"I gather you came down because you're hungry?" said Corun. "That's logical now that you're cured of the gastroparesis."

"Yeah, you probably want what Elek has to serve," Beryl said with a waggle of his brows.

"We'll leave you two to it," Kimber said, grabbing Beryl by the scruff of his neck and crab-walking him to the doorway.

"I can put a sock on the kitchen door if that'll—" Beryl's words were cut off as his two older brothers shoved him through the doorway and shut the door behind them.

"I apologize for that juvenile display," Elek said to Lily.

He had hoped that his brother's childish antics would go over her head. He wasn't so lucky. Lily was as bright as she was beautiful.

There was a light blush on her cheeks. She

fidgeted, shifting from bare foot to bare foot. She wouldn't meet his gaze.

"I'm used to guys behaving badly," she said. Her head jerked as soon as the last word left her lips. "Not that your brothers have behaved badly. They've been nothing but kind and accommodating. I'm not complaining."

The distress in her eyes bothered Elek. He wanted to pull her close and breathe his calm into her. And once he had her close, he would taste the salt that collected just under her chin.

Elek gave himself another shake. He exhaled again, trying to suffocate the beast for that wayward thought. "You're hungry."

All signs of discomfort left her features. Her mouth split into a beautiful grin. "Always," she said, coming towards him.

Elek couldn't take his eyes off her mouth. He wanted to place the sweetest treat he had to offer between her lips. He shook himself again, but the thought had taken root inside his mind.

He loved watching her eat. Loved the sounds she made when she tried a new dish of his. He loved experiencing her pleasure with his food.

"Can I try?" Lily pointed to the platter of sand-wiches on the counter.

"No."

She blinked at him. The hand that had pointed to the food curled into a loose fist that she gathered against her chest.

"I mean, this is for the girls. They're going on a shopping spree in the fae town later."

"Oh, right." Lily looked out the window. In her gaze, Elek saw the same longing that she'd had the first time he'd set a tray of food before her. She'd been surprised and delighted at the first bite when she realized she could keep the food down.

"You can't go out until I mark you," he said.

"I know," she said. "I don't mind staying inside a while longer. I know you're not ready."

She might know that he wasn't ready. She didn't know *why* he wasn't ready. He supposed he should show her the reason he was so reluctant to do his duty—as his brothers had put it. Lily should know the danger of being bound to the beast within him.

"Lily, I want you to meet my mother."

o man had ever brought her home. No man had ever asked her to meet anyone except another man that he wanted to parade her around to boost his ego to have a model on his arm. Elek didn't care about any of that. He didn't care what she looked like. He was always preoccupied with making sure she was fed, and keeping her safe.

They climbed a long and winding staircase at the back of the castle. Elek had Lily precede him. She didn't worry for a second that he was checking her ass out—he wasn't that kind of man.

Then there was a twinge that he wasn't checking her ass out because he wasn't that kind of man. Did

Elek not like women? Was that his hesitation in claiming her?

Not that she wanted the sexual bedsport she assumed went along with being claimed by a virile dragon shifter. Not that any of her sexual sport had been in a bed. The few men who had tackled Lily's lady parts had done so mostly on a couch, a few times atop a cluttered desk, and once in a urinal. Not a single one of those recreational breaks had been memorable. Not enough to keep score. Though if she was to do a tally, she would definitely be at zero.

So, if Elek wasn't playing for her team, it wouldn't be the end of the world. In fact, it would be a great time out. She and Elek could let others play the game while they sat in the stands eating the best snacks.

"It's the second door on your right," Elek said from behind her.

Lily reached for the slightly cracked door, only to realize she was about to meet Elek's mother empty-handed. Wasn't it protocol to bring the mother of the guy you were mating-but-not-dating a gift? But Elek had insisted on carrying each tray of food.

"Go on inside," Elek encouraged.

"Is she expecting us?"

Elek paused, pursing his lips. "No."

"Does she know about me?"

He breathed through his nose and exhaled the same answer. "No."

Lily put her back to the door, her voice rose in a panicked whisper. "So, we're springing this on her? Our…."

She motioned between their two chests. She certainly didn't know how to complete that sentence. She wished Elek would finish it for her so that she'd know exactly where she stood with him.

"I'm not the man you think I am, Lily," he said, putting his back to the door. "I want you to meet my mother so that you have a better understanding of that."

With a slight push, the door swung open. The room inside was dark, even though the sun was now up. There were voices coming from within the room — more than one. One of those voices was singing.

Lily found the source of the musical number—it came from the television hanging on the wall. Opposite the television was a large four-poster bed. The bed was larger than a California King. However, there was a small woman lying in the center of the mattress.

She didn't turn as Elek came into the room. Her eyes were open. Her gaze was on the television set, staring unblinkingly.

Lily walked a few steps into the room and waited for Elek's mother to acknowledge their presence. She realized she didn't know the woman's name. She supposed that would be corrected when Elek introduced them.

"Hello, Mom," said Elek.

Lily folded her hands in front of her primly, trying to look like a proper girlfriend or mate. She wasn't sure what either looked like. Her sister was always fawning all over Ilia. So were the other girls. The only time Elek touched Lily was to pass her a plate of food.

She knew she wasn't dressed to impress. She still wore the sweats. Her feet were bare. She didn't have on a lick of makeup, not even lip gloss. She couldn't be making a good impression. That had to be the reason Elek's mother didn't even acknowledge her presence.

"I've brought you a treat tonight. Berry nectar with a hint of mint." Elek grabbed a plastic bag from the tray of food. Reaching to the side of the bed, he unscrewed an empty bag from an IV and went about screwing in the new bag.

That's when Lily realized it wasn't that his mother was ignoring her, it was that she couldn't respond. "She's catatonic."

Elek didn't respond. He didn't need to. Lily had been in this state more times in her life than she cared to count. The difference was, it lasted for a few moments, twenty minutes at the most.

Whenever she went to a casting call, she lost herself inside her own body. It was much like having a witch on her back, except she hadn't gone to sleep first. Looking at Elek's mother, Lily recognized the woman as the same.

"Hello," said Lily as she came to stand by the bed. "I'm Lily. I'm Elek's...."

Once again, she looked for Elek to guide her. He was arranging the sheets around his mother, not meeting Lily's gaze. Elek's mother hadn't taken her eyes off the television.

Lily sat gingerly on the bed. She reached out to the unblinking woman. With trembling fingers, Lily rested her hand atop the older woman's.

Her hands were warm to the touch, which was unexpected. Lily always felt cold during and after she came out of one of her spells. There was no struggle in the woman's dark gaze. There was no emotion at all.

"What's her name?" Lily asked.

"Miyaoaxochitl. Miya for short. But we all call her Mom."

"How long has she been like this?"

"Since I was ten."

"How…?" Lily let the question die on her lips. A chill raced across her shoulder blades, whispering the answer. A moment later, Elek confirmed her fears.

"It is my fault. I did this to her." His gaze lifted to hers. There was a cool glow of amber in his hazel eyes. Lily felt like she was looking at more than Elek the man. She saw inside him to the beast within.

Her heart began to race. The thudding beats did not resound in fear. She felt the ache of compassion for both the little boy who had lost his mother, and the beast who blamed itself.

"My father…was hurting her." Elek's eyes burned brighter as the memory took hold of him. "I was too small to protect her, and so I let my beast out. My beast is very large, even when I was young. I managed to beat my father down, but in doing so, I…."

Lily let go of Elek's mother and reached for his hand. Unlike his mother, Elek's hands were cold.

Lily clutched at his fingers with hers, trying to impart her warmth to him.

"You saved her," she said.

"Her life, yes. But this," his gaze fell to his prone mother, "is no way to live."

Elek turned his hand over, capturing her fingers in his. It was the first time he'd willingly touched her without offering her food. The coldness fled his body, and all Lily felt was a warmth she wanted to wrap herself up in.

"To claim you, I'll have to let my beast loose."

Understanding dawned on Lily. "You're afraid you'll do this to me."

Elek looked down at their entwined fingers. The amber light in his eyes dimmed with shame. He began to pull away from her, but Lily held fast.

"Elek, we don't have to—"

"We do. If you want to have a life here, we do. I will not trap another woman inside this castle."

"Okay," Lily soothed. "But tonight we can just Netflix and chill."

Elek frowned at those words.

"We can just eat snacks and watch television with your mom."

Some of the tension left his face. His eyes didn't

return to their soft hazel. There was still an amber glow around his irises.

"I've been working since I was an infant. I'm due for a staycation. Can I pick the show?"

A tentative smile spread across Elek's face. "As long as I get to pick the snacks."

"Deal."

CHAPTER FIVE

he beat of *The Rhythm of the Night* sounded from the television set in his mother's room. Elek had never been one for lively tunes, preferring the natural sounds of rushing water, gentle winds, and chimes. But he bopped his head along to the beat of the musical group DeBarge.

Aside from the beat, the lyrics of the song called to him as well. The encouraged listeners to forget about the worries on the their minds and leave them behind. That was how Elek preferred to live his life.

On the other side of the bed, Lily bobbed her head to the tune. She lifted first her right and then her left shoulder in time to the beat, a small smile of enjoyment on her face. As she shook her shoulders, she appeared to shake off all the blues of her past away. If Cardi were here watching the film *The Last Dragon* with them, she would have dubbed *The Rhythm of the Night* Elek and Lily's song. Elek decided he liked the idea of having a shared song with Lily.

The song died down and another fight scene played out on the small screen. The movie's hero—Bruce Leeroy—came face-to-face with the film's villain, Sho'nuff. Being the true hero that he was, Leroy declined to fight the man. That was, until his lady love was kidnapped and put in harm's way by the villain.

Inside his belly, Elek's dragon sat up. A low growl rumbled up into his chest as the damsel was tied up and handled roughly. The beast insisted Elek turn his gaze to Lily.

She sat safely and securely on the bed. She leaned toward Mom as she popped the sweet treats he'd made for her into her mouth, one by one. The beast stared out through Elek's eyes at Lily's lush lips. It wasn't just his belly that stirred.

Elek shut his eyes, calling for calm. It would be a losing battle if he had to contend with not one, but two of his lower beasts.

Another blast from the television jerked him out

of his contemplation. Sho'nuff had Leroy cornered. The martial arts fighting between the two had been evenly matched. Until Sho'nuff exhibited that he had the masterful power of The Glow.

Lily gripped Mom's arm as Sho'nuff got in blow after blow on Leroy. The treats were forgotten. Her wide eyes were full of disbelief and agony as Sho'nuff fixed his bushy hair and prepared for the kill-strike that would take the hero down.

Elek palmed the remote, ready to do the most damage to the story by turning the film off. Especially when tears glistened in Lily's eyes. Sho'nuff's glowing red hands struck Leroy repeatedly, egging the hero on to admit that Sho'nuff was the true master.

Lily lay her head on his mother's shoulder. The movement caused his mother's head to dip and rest atop Lily's. Mom blinked unseeingly at the screen. Elek swore for a second he'd seen her chest heave with a sigh.

On the screen, the hero was being dunked repeatedly in water. Over and over again, the villain demanded that Leroy call him the true master of kung fu, red sparks flying from his hands. Lily sat forward, her shoulders tensed. Until they relaxed, when a golden glow began to emit from the hero.

Lily pressed her hands to her chest as Leroy windmilled his arms, bringing all the light-giving power of a true master to defeat his enemy. Elek had seen this movie hundreds of times, but watching it with Lily for the first time, he was breathless with anticipation. With Leroy's super mastery, he defeated the villainous Sho'nuff…only to come face to face with another obstacle that appeared to end his life, leaving the heroine to face a world without him.

"I should've seen that coming," said Lily, gathering her knees to her chest. "Heroes can never have love."

"The film isn't over," Elek said. "The hero will triumph."

"Sure." Lily heaved a sigh. "In the movies."

"You don't believe love is possible in the real world?" asked Elek.

"Not like that." Lily straightened out her legs and scooted until her back rested against the headboard.

On the screen, Leroy and the heroine reunited. He'd survived the final attack, and the two were now engaged in a searing lip-lock.

Lily picked up the bowl of treats, but didn't put any to her mouth. "Well, except for my sister and your brother. And the other women and dragons. But that's happened here, in this world."

"You're here in this world now."

She didn't say anything for a time as she watched the credits of the film roll. Once the words finished their upward scroll, she turned to Elek. "I don't expect you to love me."

The dragon inside him wanted to roar. It wanted to protest. Elek kept it quiet. He, of all people, knew that he could never love Lily in the same way that his brothers loved their mates. He simply wasn't capable of it.

"The only person I've ever loved who loved me back without strings or ultimatums is my sister. I don't understand how you can feel it for someone who isn't a part of you."

Elek wondered at that? Did he love his brothers? He knew he loved his mother. Although that feeling always sat heavy in his chest, the weight of guilt dragging it down.

"I think love is just something men tell women to get in their pants."

Elek choked at Lily's words.

Lily lifted her gaze, but she didn't look at him. She rearranged the collar of Mom's nightgown and tucked the covers more tightly around her waist.

"I care about you, Lily."

"I know."

"I will protect you."

"I know that, too. I'm grateful." Finally, she allowed her gaze to meet his. "It's more than I ever expected from a man."

"I'm sorry I can't give you more."

"You feed me," she said with a grin. "Your mastery of cooking fills my belly and that's the organ that has an appetite in me. Not my heart."

"I am no master."

"You sure look like a master to me."

Elek chuckled at her recitation of the lines from the film they'd just watched. He didn't often have occasion to laugh, but he found himself doing it more and more with Lily in his life.

"There you are," said Rose, barging into the room. "I knew if you weren't in the kitchen, you'd be in here watching shows and movies."

Elek and Lily had been Netflix and chilling for over a week. Though they still hadn't watched the film or television show called Netflix.

"We're headed out to a fae fashion show," said Cardi. "It's not as cute as 80s fashion. But the material they use is, like, to die for."

There was another of Cardi's terms he didn't get.

Family and honor were the only things Elek could fathom that were worth dying for. Not an article of fabric.

Lily perked up at the word *fashion*. Elek knew females loved to adorn themselves in bright clothes and shining accessories. It was clear Lily wanted to do the same.

"That sounds like fun," said Lily, her sedate tone at odds with the light of desire in her eyes.

"We want you to come with us," said Rose, grabbing hold of her sister's hands.

"There'll be other shifters there," said Cardi. "Elek will need to mark you before we go."

"Oh." The light in Lily's gaze dimmed. "No, that's okay. I don't really need any new clothing."

"You've been wearing the same oversized t-shirt and sweats for three days now," said Rose. "If there were fashion police here, they would've thrown the book at you."

"And then stuffed you at the back of the closet," added Cardi.

"I'll go next time," Lily said.

At Lily's response, Cardi and Rose glared at Elek.

There was a part of Elek that didn't want Lily to go because he wanted her to stay with him and keep Netflixing and chilling. But a larger part of him realized he was keeping Lily trapped in this room. Just as his mother was trapped in here.

"You should go with them," he said. "I'll mark you now."

Cardi and Rose looked triumphant. Lily looked surprised. Mom stared straight ahead at the blank television. Inside Elek, the dragon sharpened its claws.

CHAPTER SIX

"It's gonna hurt," said Cardi.

"But not hurt-hurt," said Chryssie. "More like the loss of virginity hurt."

"When I lost my V-card with Kimber, that did not hurt."

"Yeah, same with Corun."

Cardi and Chryssie turned their dreamy gazes to Poppy. Poppy's hand, as well as her gaze, rested on her round belly. It took a moment of the silence before she looked up to add her two cents.

"Oh, my first time hurt. But it was with a human. So..." She shrugged.

Cardi and Chryssie both wrinkled their nose at the notion of losing it to a human. Lily could agree.

"It wasn't like he was big or anything," Poppy

went on. "He just didn't know what he was doing. Or he didn't care."

"My first was a human, and he knew what he was doing," said Rose. Her gaze wasn't dreamy and far-off with the memory, as Cardi's and Chryssie's had been. "But it still hurt."

Lily didn't want to think back to her first time. Mainly because she didn't remember it too well. She remembered laying chest down over the back of a couch. There had been a stain on the wall; long and skinny like water had dripped from a pipe above. The water had pooled in one section, leaving behind a brown spot.

As her virginity had been pounded out of her, she'd heard a toilet flush above. The pipes had rattled and clanked. Instead of wondering if that was the source of the leak, Lily had retreated into her mind.

She'd stayed trapped there for moments after the sex was over. Sometimes, even if she was wide awake, the paralysis gripped her. After he'd zipped up his pants, her deflowerer had slapped her bare ass and told her to head to the dressing room to be fitted. That had snapped her out of it. She remembered the sting of his hand more than anything else, including his name.

"There's something in a dragon's bite that acts like a drug," Chryssie was saying. "Corun tried to explain it to me. Something about endorphins, and the nervous system, and...something. I stopped listening and started kissing him. I get all riled up when he goes hot-scientist on me."

"Yeah," said Cardi. "It's like a drug or something. It makes you feel really good every time they do it."

"Kimber still bites you?" asked Lily.

"Oh, yeah." Cardi grinned. "Right when he's about to you...you know."

Lily supposed she knew what Cardi meant, though she and Elek wouldn't be having sex. It wasn't something either of them wanted from this relationship.

They were just friends. Which was nice. Lily had never had a guy friend before. She'd had guys say they wanted to be her friend, and then they'd schemed to get in her panties.

Not Elek. He'd promised to protect her, and he'd done nothing but that since the day they'd met. Though, if he had asked her for sex, Lily would've obliged. It was the least she could do for all he'd done for her. All he was doing for her.

Not only was Elek keeping her safe, but he'd also given her a place where she belonged. The dragons and their mates had given her and her sister a family who cared about them. And Elek filled her belly every day with the most delicious food.

If he wanted to dip his stick in a few times, Lily would lie back and think of all the pie he'd make for her afterward. It wouldn't be a big deal. It would just be sex.

Lily descended the stairs from her room quietly. She had thought Elek would've wanted to do it in his bedroom. Or her bedroom. Instead, he'd asked her to meet him in the kitchen when she was ready.

From outside the door, the most scrumptious smells wafted towards her. Lily stopped for a moment and simply inhaled. Her belly no longer grumbled, not now that it knew the sensation of satisfaction.

Her entire body felt full, from her head to her fingertips, on down to her toes. Lily had not a care in the world. Nowhere to go and be seen. No one to impress or beg for sustenance. Nothing and nobody in this world would hurt her. And that would be doubly true once she received Elek's mark.

Inside the kitchen, pots boiled on the stove. Something sweet rose in a tin inside the oven. Elek bent down over the hearth. His large hands drew lazy circles inside a dark cauldron.

She knew he sensed her presence—he always did. He doused the flame and stood. But he didn't turn to her.

"Hey," Lily said.

Elek nodded in acknowledgement, but did not raise his gaze. He shifted from foot to foot, placing his hands in the pockets of his flowing pants. He stole a quick glance at her, and then immediately looked the other way.

Lily hated his unease. All week they had been nothing but chummy. But they'd often had Mom between them, or a series of ingredients and mixing bowls. Now they stood facing each other.

"Elek, we don't have to—"

"Stand there." He pointed to the island at the center of the kitchen.

Lily moved aside the various barstools. She turned her back to Elek and braced her hands on the cool marble. It brought to mind the couch from her first time. Though there were no stains on the walls. Instead of piping sounds, the crackle of fire and gurgle of cooking stews filled the room.

"Do you want me to undress?" she asked.

"Why would you undress?"

Lily opened her mouth and then closed it. None of the girls had said anything about undressing for the first bite. But she supposed he had to get to her flesh somehow and she *was* covered in an oversized t-shirt.

"We are not having sexual intercourse, Lily. Our relationship is not like my brothers' and their mates'. I have control over my dragon. I don't need a mate… in that way. The mark is for your protection."

"I understand. I'm sorry."

She should've felt relief. In a way, she did. But there was something niggling at the back of her neck.

Lily looked over her shoulder. Elek stood just behind her, his large body only an inch from hers. They had never been this close before, not even when he spoon-fed her samples of his cooking.

"Where will you…mark me?" she asked.

"Your shoulder. On your clavicle, so that it can be seen by others."

Elek's gaze focused on that spot. It was only just barely visible beneath the collar of the T-shirt.

Lily reached up with both her hands. With her right hand, she swept her hair over her shoulder. With her left hand, she tugged at the collar to give him more room to work with.

Elek stepped an inch closer. The heat of his body lifted the temperature of the room a half dozen degrees. His hands hovered over her without touching, but she could make out each one of his fingers. When his fingers touched her flesh, she felt her blood rise like mercury in a thermometer.

Lily heard Elek give an audible gulp. And then a growl. Both sounds reverberated through her. First the wetness of the gulp, followed by the rumble of the growl.

The mercury in the thermometer of her body burst when she felt his hot breath on her neck. Lily closed her eyes, breathing in Elek's scent of spice and fire.

He gave her no warning of his bite. One moment, all she felt was heat. The next she felt two sharp pin-pricks. She did feel pain. But only for a split second, and likely more from the surprise of it than anything else.

After the sharpness, there was a sweetness that followed. Like hot honey. It should've burned. It should've scalded her flesh. Instead, it felt like being submerged in a bubble bath at the end of a long day. No, not a day, a long week. Maybe even a month.

The warmth slid from her neck and down to her chest. Her nipples pebbled to tight points. The slick heat of Elek's bite flowed down to her stomach, which ached with a hunger that she knew food would not satisfy.

Down the warmth spread until it reached her legs. Lily felt the need to move her hips as it made its way to her center. The heat was gathering like she'd seen tidal waves do. The wave rose and rushed to the center of her.

Lily's hands dug into the countertop. Her body began to tremble. But she did not move. Not while Elek held her fast to his body.

She felt the strength of his chest against her spine and her back arched. She felt the heat of his lips against her neck and her knees buckled. She felt the outline of a throbbing erection against her ass and her core pulsed.

It was sensation overload. The flood gates of desire would open if one more thing—

Elek's tongue licked at her flesh. That was all it took. Explosions went off inside of Lily. The pulsations rocked her up onto her tippy toes, up onto her fingertips. Her upper body crashed down onto the top of the island. Her breasts hit the cool marble.

The tidal wave flung her out to sea. The wave pulled her under and then back onto dry land. Only to lift her up and send her back down into the deep.

Lily surfaced, gasping for air with her lungs.

Desperate to be filled between her legs. Aching to be held against something strong and sure.

There was no one there. Elek was no longer at her neck. No longer at her back. She only came back to her senses when she heard the splintering crash of shattering glass. She opened her eyes to see a dragon flying out of the window.

It took Lily some time before she could stand on her own feet. Her hand went to the bite mark. There was no blood, but she felt the raised skin. She also felt a pinprick of pain at her shoulders. Glancing down at her forearms, she saw scratches from claws. Running her finger over the marks, she felt the heat pulse once more inside of her.

The mark made her safe. The clawmarks made her feel wanted. She realized something she'd never expected to feel in her life, something she'd never thought she could.

Lily wanted Elek.

# CHAPTER SEVEN

*A*nimals darted out of his way, both large and small. A bale of turtles ducked into their shells, leaving their hard exteriors exposed to the danger. A herd of hairy legged mastodons, that had been striding steadily forward, all took giant steps back, sharp tusks angling away from Elek and his beast.

Branches cracked from tree trunks as man and beast swung their arms, trying to wrestle control. Roots were torn up as sharp claws and calloused toes tussled for purchase on the ground. A flock of pterodactyls dispersed in the sky as Elek's wings tore from his back and he leaped into the air.

The beast wanted out. The beast wanted to turn

back, crash into the kitchen window and claim what was his. The beast wanted Lily.

For years, the animal inside Elek had sat quietly, sedately. Its maw had hung low in shame and guilt. Elek realized that had all been a ruse. The animal had simply been biding its time.

The taste of Lily was still on his lips. Still at the underside of his teeth. The essence of her had gone down his throat and was now lodged in his belly, in his gut.

The need to sink his teeth into her, to sink his claws into her, to sink other parts of himself into her was almost too strong to resist. Almost.

The overwhelming desire to claim her had nearly taken over his mind. Nearly.

The dragon's impulse to ravage Lily had all but conquered Elek's will. But Elek was not a man to be easily diverted. He knew that the best way to win against a rising tide was to surrender to it. And so he gave the dragon his body.

His soft human flesh hardened until amber scales gleamed in the bright sun. Short pale fingernails gave over to claws as dark, and as hard, as jade. His wings extended fully from his back, expanding wide enough to temporarily block out the sun from the forest creatures below.

The dragon could move fast. The dragon could fly high. The dragon could put the most amount of distance between himself and Lily.

When the dragon realized that he was flying in the wrong direction, the beast roared. Elek allowed the animal its fit. He'd given his other half control over his body, but he maintained a firm grip on his mind. And where the mind directed, so the body went.

His flight turned turbulent as the war raged inside him. His hind legs clipped treetops. His head narrowly missed a hilltop.

The will to live was strong, and the beast stopped its thrashing for a brief moment to allow them to land. Once grounded, it took up the fight again. The dragon tried to make a run for it. Back to the castle. Back to her. Back to that taste.

Animals darted in front of him, so confused by the normally stealth dragon's crashing and crunching. Elek could've picked them off for a whole meal. The thought of anything on his tongue that wasn't *her* was abhorrent.

He wanted the salt of her skin. He wanted the suppleness of her flesh. He wanted the sweetness he'd found in her blood. He wanted the pleasure of that cry she'd made when he'd pursed his lips and pulled—

No. Not him. He didn't want those things.

It was the dragon inside of him. It was the dragon whose loins had tightened at the taste of her. It was the dragon who had growled at her low moan.

He knew it hadn't been a cry of pain or fear. It had been a cry of desire. She had wanted him, too. It was the last thing Elek had expected.

Neither he nor Lily wanted a physical relationship. It was the dragon that had brought carnality into their friendship. Elek would not let the beast have her. It was far too unpredictable, too volatile.

It had crippled his mother, sending her so deeply into the recesses of her mind that she could never return. That must never happen again.

He would not do that to Lily. Lily who was vibrant. She was also fragile. One wrong move from his massive beast and she would not survive it. The thought of her eyes going glassy made the beast shudder.

Finally, man and beast were of one mind. Neither wanted harm to come to Lily. That shudder was enough to give Elek the upper hand.

He willed his body to retract its wings. But the

dragon roared, flapping its wings and sending more birds into the air.

Elek clenched his fists, trying to retract his claws. The dragon dug the sharp points into his palms, drawing blood.

Elek took a deep inhale in an attempt to slow his breathing. His heart raced as the dragon fought to stay present.

Finally, Elek shut his eyes. But all he could see was Lily. Lily's pink cheeks. Lily's soft curves. Lily's lips as she hummed while eating a dish he'd prepared for her.

Everything in him tightened. His loins. His claws. His heart.

No matter what he did, Elek couldn't regain the control he'd prized himself for having.

*Dragon's needed mates*, the gnarled voice in his head demanded. That mark on Lily's neck made her his. He should do what the Goddess intended all beasts to do. Sink himself into his mate's warm flesh until she screamed with pleasure.

Elek dug his claws into the ground, intent on not allowing the beast to go anywhere. He was far enough away from the castle. All around, he smelled the super sweetness of fairies.

But on the horizon, he caught the hot-honey scent of Lily. Was he going mad? Or was she near?

He looked up to see the banners for the fair. That's when he remembered why he'd marked Lily today. He remembered where she had gone. Elek couldn't grab the reins of the beast fast enough. It slipped his tightly held leash and bounded for the fair, for his mate.

CHAPTER EIGHT

The fabrics were unlike anything Lily had ever seen on a runway, in a department store, or even in a sewing room. Some glowed, like rays of sunlight had been woven into the thread. Others shimmered with sparkling particles of dust.

"It's fairy dust," Chryssie told her.

The willowy fairies who sewed the designs would be a hit on New York fashion catwalks. Their lithe bodies would put sample-size garments to shame and make every male designer with unrealistic expectations of women's bodies salivate. Lily wondered if fairies were the inspiration behind most designs. The average human woman was a size twelve, which would fit three or four fairies into a dress's pocket.

Speaking of sample size, Lily hadn't fit into the outfit she'd first tried on. In less than two weeks, she'd gone from a size zero to a whopping size three. In her life before, she would've felt nothing but shame for the flesh flowing over the waistband of the garment. There was a ringing in her ear as she waited for the designer to yell at her for gaining a few extra pounds.

"Just give it a second," said the fairy fashionista.

After a second, the fabric began to move and shift. It filled out at the space around her hips and pulled at her midsection. In less than a moment, the dress had fit itself to her form, highlighting her best assets while hiding her flaws. The fit was beyond what any tailor could have ever achieved.

Lily looked in the mirror and marveled. She had gained weight in the last few days. It was visible. But she didn't look like a landed whale. She looked healthy with her curves filled out. Her chest didn't sink in. Her cheeks were pink. And then there was the mark on her neck.

The fairy stared too, not bothering to hide her interest. "You're Elek's woman?"

Lily wasn't sure what to say to that? Was she Elek's woman? The man had bitten her and then run away from her. Or rather, he'd crashed out a window and flew away.

"Shame what the Goddess did to the beasts," said the fairy. She gave a shake of her lilac curls. The tendrils of her hair gave off a scent that no flowers on earth could ever match. "At least She left fairies mates."

The fairy looked over at a male in the corner. The ebony-skinned fae with green tufts of hair grinned. She gave him a wink. The room filled with enough floral perfume to make Lily feel lightheaded.

"So will you be taking that?" asked the purple-haired fairy.

Lily wanted the garment. Despite the comfort of the t-shirts and sweats she'd been luxuriating in since she'd gotten here, she missed dressing up. This dress fit her body in a way other clothes never would. But then she realized that she didn't have any money.

"Yes, she will," said Cardi. "She looks fabulous in it. Though I'd add a bit of fringe."

The purple haired fairy winced at the notion of fringe, but she fixed her face before Cardi glanced up. Cardi's own jeans were covered in multicolored fringe. Another woman would've been mocked as she walked down the street, but Cardi pulled it off.

"Cardi, I don't have any money."

"Yes, you do. You're rich. We're all rich."

If that was a fact, no one had bothered to inform Lily's pockets. In fact, the sweats she'd been wearing didn't have any pockets. She hadn't even thought to bring a purse with her. Not that there would've been any money in it either.

"I don't have any cash," said Lily.

"No one takes Benjamins here. Gems are the currency. Dragons mine gems."

Cardi put her hand to her neck. It dripped with diamonds. A diamond necklace with a heart-shaped pendant. Diamond earrings hung from her lobes. On her finger was the largest iced rock Lily had ever seen.

"Kimmy mines diamonds. Elek mines amber. Just put it on Elek's tab, Starla."

"I don't think Elek has a tab," said Starla, the fairy. "He's never shopped here before. Or had any fairy shop here for herself."

Lily had been about to argue over using Elek's money as her own when that last little bit called her up short. Elek had never bought anything for another woman? She would be his first?

"Then start one for him," said Cardi. "Me and my

new sisters are going to do some serious damage today."

Starla gave a purple-lashed wink at Lily and went behind the counter. Lily's gaze followed her there and landed on a charm. The intricate design reminded her of the talisman Bruce Leeroy's Master had given him in the film.

Cardi and Lily left the shop with bags full. There was a pep in Lily's step. There was a lightness in her heart. There was still the throb at her neck where Elek had marked her.

Lily reached up to touch the mark. Before her hand could get there, her sister hooked her arm through Lily's. Rose grinned over at her sister. Lily had never seen this light of happiness in her sister's eyes as long as they'd been alive. It was all because she'd been claimed by a dragon shifter who loved her fiercely.

The fullness Lily had felt these past couple of weeks seemed to shrivel in the light of Rose's glow. Suddenly, the savory treats and sweet desserts weren't enough. Lily wanted more from this life.

"Who invited human sluts to the fair?"

A menagerie of fairies strolled towards them. Orange-haired and pink-faced. Blue-haired and lavender-faced. Raven-haired and pale-skinned.

They looked like a girl-gang stepping out of *Marie Claire*, but the scowls on their faces turned them ugly.

"Shut up," Cardi sang sweetly, coming to stand beside Lily, "or I'll snap you like a twig."

The threat was enough to ruffle their petals. The fairies gave the humans a wide berth, but their whispered insults carried back to Lily's ears.

"Ignore them," said Chryssie. "They're just jealous they can't mate with shifters. They can only screw them."

"And now there are no dragons left for them to screw," said Cardi.

"Why can't shifters and fairies mate?" Lily asked.

"Not compatible," said Chryssie. "They're two different species, so they can't make babies, and that's the prime directive of the Goddess."

Would Elek want a baby with her? Did Lily want a baby? She wasn't sure. She hadn't wanted sex until she'd felt Elek's mouth on her neck.

"Wow," came a gentle roar. "Elek marked you, I see. He marked you hard."

Lily looked up. And then up some more. A golden-haired god blocked out the sun. The man looked like a body builder with the head of a lion.

Golden blond hair radiated from his crown. His eyes shifted from brown to golden, and back again.

"You're right, Leander," agreed Cardi. She spoke to the lion man, but her gaze latched onto Lily's neck. "I didn't want to say anything, but it is pretty impressive."

Lily's hand went to her neck. The feel of the raised skin there sent a shiver of warmth straight to the core of her. She had the urge to close her eyes and get lost in the memory of Elek behind her, pulling her close as he sank into her.

"He still hasn't mated you." Leander's nostrils flared as he inhaled. "You don't have his scent."

Those brown-and-golden eyes flashed a bright yellow and stayed that way. Lily felt like a gazelle cornered by the king of the jungle. She felt the ice creeping up her spine. Then a roar sent the shivers away, leaving behind only warmth.

But the lion hadn't opened his mouth. *He* hadn't roared. Lily turned and saw fairies scrambling out of the path as an amber-colored dragon landed in the clearing.

Elek.

CHAPTER NINE

*R*ed.

That's all Elek saw as he glared at the beast who had his mate cornered. He knew the overgrown pussycat had a name, but Elek was having trouble accessing any rational thought, and that included his memories.

All he saw was red. Even though the lion was a bright golden-yellow. The sight would've made Elek wince had it not been for all the red in his vision. He needed more red to mute the annoying yellow. The lion's blood would do.

"Calm down there, E." The lion's voice was not a roar. It was a low purr. More the sound of a house cat seeking attention than the king of the jungle bellowing a command.

Elek's ears heard the rational request. His eyes saw the gleam of sharp, white teeth. Teeth that were close enough to sink into Lily's flesh.

"I did not touch your mate."

The lion held up his hands. They were large hands. At the tips and all along the index finger were inky black spots, as though the animal spent much of his time writing.

Elek knew a lion who spent most days with a pen in his hand. Leander was his name. This Leander wrote awful poetry, but the words always came from the heart. His pure heart. His kind heart. Because Leander was a friendly lion.

A friendly lion that wanted to get his dirty paws on Elek's mate and assault her ears with bad rhyme.

Red curtained Elek's vision. He unballed his fingers from the fists he'd clenched. His claws came out with a *cling*.

The lion cursed under his breath. "You should think about this."

Elek swung. Leander leaped up and back, easily evading Elek's strike.

"You've always been the calm one of that weyr."

Those words from the poet rang true. Much of Elek's skill had come as a result of the calm he'd cultivated over the years. He took a deep, cleansing breath and swung again.

"Elek, we're friends." Leander ducked, only just evading the tip of Elek's index claw. "If you want to keep that distinction, you're going to need to stah—"

The next punch connected. The sound of thudding flesh and bones crunching was good to Elek's ears. The sight of the blood soothed him, it muted the annoying golden-yellow emitting from his foe.

"Are you going to make me have to slap some sense into you, old friend?"

Golden eyes shone even brighter, irritating the raging beast within Elek. A trickle of blood ran from Leander's flaring nostrils to his upper lip. That slow trickle of red dimmed the bloodthirsty haze in Elek's mind.

The lion was down on one knee, but he wasn't out. Leander whipped his head back, and the golden mane fell over his shoulders. Behind him, many of the fairies sighed. One may have swooned at the hair show.

"I told you, I'm not after your girl."

A glance over his shoulder told Elek where Lily was. But that glance showed Elek that her eyes were wide. Her arms were wrapped tight around her body. The smell of fear came off her.

She was frightened. But of what? It had to have been the lion that had frightened her.

His overlarge body. His massive bulk. His uncontained rage.

*That's you,* a small voice whispered inside Elek's mind. The voice was familiar. It sounded like his own.

Looking down at himself, Elek saw that he was still partially shifted. Orange scales extended halfway up his forearms. He felt the sharp fangs of the dragon's teeth cutting into his lower lip. His wings were out, though not extended to their full length.

Neither man nor beast were fully in control. Which meant he was entirely out of control. The internal war that had been raging inside of him had spilled over and was now hurting the people he cared about.

He'd bloodied Leander. He'd frightened Lily. He'd lost himself.

A roar tore up from his gut and escaped his lips. The cry of pain and frustration was powerful enough to shake the tops of the trees.

Unfortunately, the other beings around took his cry for help as a battle cry. Fairies scurried out of the way and dove for cover. Rose put a protective arm around her sister. Lily still hadn't moved. She remained frozen, staring in muted horror at Elek.

All of Elek's and the dragon's defenses went down. That's when the lion charged.

With a roar, Leander crashed into Elek. Elek's wings extended on reflex. The dragon wanted to gut the lion with its claws. Elek managed to curl those deadly weapons into fists and keep his friend alive. Still, he had to defend himself.

Elek kicked out a foot. He caught Leander on the shin. The lion threw a fist and caught Elek in the solar plexus. And then the whole world stopped.

It was slight. Barely audible. But he heard it. Elek heard Lily whimper.

It was enough to loosen the dragon's leash and bring the man back to the forefront of control.

"Enough!" Elek bellowed, holding out his large human hand with claws retracted.

Either it was the soft human flesh in face of a lion's jaw, or something in his face must've communicated that things were over. Leander backpedaled, windmilling his arms in an almost comical fashion until he came to a halt.

"You you again?" asked the lion.

Elek ignored the question. Instead, he rushed to

Lily. Yet when he was within touching distance of her, he fumbled.

She had sunken into herself. Literally and physically. Her eyes were the same glassy expression his mother wore on a daily basis. Her shoulders were hunched. Her fingers trembled.

Inside his belly, the dragon whined a pitiful sound. It was a sound Elek had heard before. The shame and guilt it had felt when he'd accidentally hurt his mother.

Elek stood before the last person in the world he wanted to hurt. The person he wanted to raise up high on a pedestal and protect. Lily stared right through him as though she didn't see him, or didn't know who he was. Until finally, she blinked.

"I want to go home," she said.

That was enough to put Elek into motion. He wrapped her up in his arms. Without hesitation, the dragon gave over his wings. Up in the air they went with Lily cradled in his arms.

s Elek wrapped his arms around her, Lily felt the heat from before infusing her. She barely noticed when his skin turned to scales. She didn't blink when dark wings grew from his back and stretched so far and wide that it blocked out every other living person from sight. She kept staring into his amber-colored eyes and only saw Elek, the man. Elek, who promised to protect her.

Nearly every day of her life before this, men had pawed at her. Pinched her. Groped her. And she'd allowed it. She'd had to for her and her sister's sustenance.

Elek had opened his arms to her, giving her a choice. Lily had only taken half a step, but it was enough. No, it was more than enough. For the first time, Lily felt safe in the hands of a man.

It was when she was airborne that she realized it might be a good idea to be afraid.

"I have you."

Lily looked at the dragon's face. It was Elek, but with the dragon just below the surface. His cheeks were a blend of flesh and scales. His lips stretched wide over teeth that belonged to a shark. But Lily saw Elek in those fire-bright eyes. What she didn't see was his mouth move as he spoke to her.

"Telepathy," he said without his lips moving.

Telepathy? Lily had heard of such things, but only in science-fiction stories. In reality, it was a heady experience having someone speak directly into her mind. Could he read her thoughts as well?

"Yes. It is inevitable with skin-to-skin contact. But I would never willfully invade your privacy. I would also never let you fall. It is my sole desire to be your protector, Lily."

"Then why did you leave me?" she said.

A gust of wind rocked them slightly off course. Lily threw her arms around Elek's neck and held on fast, shutting her eyes.

She'd always been a nervous flyer. Even when the

Fasten Your Seatbelt light was off, she'd kept the belt securely locked around her waist. There was no seatbelt on Air Elek. There wasn't a seat, a cockpit, or outer shell of this particular flying machine.

"I'm sorry," his words sounded in her mind. "Your words caught me off guard."

"You left me. This morning, you left after... After."

Lily looked away. Better to face the skies up above or the land down below than to stare into those bright eyes. She could avert her gaze, but while she flew in the seat of Elek's hold, he was fastened onto her mind.

"I didn't want you to be frightened of me," came his response a few heartbeats later.

Turning back to face Elek, Lily let out a breath she hadn't realized she was holding. Her hands locked behind Elek's neck. Her fingers tentatively touched the thick hair at his nape. "I wasn't frightened of you."

Elek pressed his lips together. His wings beat strong. His hold on her tightened. He wouldn't meet her eyes.

"You promised you'd never lie to me," said Lily.

Before the words left his lips, a low growl came out first. "I was frightened."

"Of me?" she asked.

"Of myself. Of the dragon. I nearly lost control of my beast this morning after… After. That has only happened once before."

Pressed so firmly against his chest, Lily felt Elek's heart pounding against her cheek. With every word that he spoke, the pace increased. Yet the look on his face remained stoic.

"It happened with your mother?" asked Lily.

Instead of nodding, Elek flared his wings. When Lily looked down again, she saw that they flew above the castle. Elek flared his wings once more, bringing them into a slow descent. They touched down at her bedroom window. His hold loosened, but he did not set her down, and Lily made no move to leave his embrace.

"That lion wasn't about to hurt me," said Lily.

Elek's look of enduring stoicism morphed into something dark and possessive. It should've frightened Lily. She'd seen that expression on the faces of other men who had wanted her body. But here, with Elek, she welcomed the dark side.

"He might not have meant to. But the pull to claim you is strong."

Slowly, carefully, Elek set Lily on her feet. He kept a hold on her until she appeared to be steady.

"Do you feel the pull to claim me?" Lily asked.

Elek didn't answer for a long while. When he spoke, it was with his voice and not from his mind to hers. "It is the dragon. His instinct is to claim you for his own."

That sent a thrill through Lily. She'd always heard that men were beasts. Here before her stood a man with the gentlest of souls. Yet inside of him was a carnal creature who wanted to sink its teeth into her. It was now Lily's heartbeat that raced.

"To do that, to claim you, I would need to give over control to the beast. Which would be unsafe for both you and me. My dragon is unpredictable. It could hurt you."

"Like with your mother."

Elek's eyes flashed at her. Lily swore it was the dragon looking out at her with burning amber eyes. The beast inside Elek blinked, and his irises went cool again. Then, only Elek looked back at her.

Lily hadn't realized before that man and beast were two separate entities. Where she often got lost and trapped inside of herself, Elek had something trapped inside of him that wanted to get out and take control.

"Why don't you get some rest?"

As though it agreed with his words, the sun

dipped lower on the horizon. The yellow orb reached muted orange rays over the treetops, like it was tucking the flora into bed. Lily stared at her own bed with trepidation.

She doubted Rose was back from the fair yet. When her sister came back, she'd likely want to show Ilia all of her new clothing. Then Ilia would likely want to rip each article off his mate. Rose wouldn't be around to check on Lily and keep the witches off her back. At the thought of the sleep paralysis, Lily's body shuddered involuntarily.

"I'm not tired," she said, walking into the bedroom and heading for the door. "Why don't we go and watch television with your mother, instead?"

"What is it?" Elek asked.

He hadn't moved from the balcony. He stood with the setting orange sun as a backdrop. The sight of him standing there, calm, strong, protective, made Lily's heart flutter. It was the flutter that allowed the truth to sneak past her lips.

"I don't sleep well alone. I get a witch on my back."

"A witch? There are no witches here. They are not allowed."

"Wait? Witches are real?"

Elek only stared, waiting patiently for an explanation.

"It's a human expression. A metaphor, I think? I get muscle spasms when I sleep. My body locks up and I can't move, even though I'm awake and conscious. I feel like I'm trapped inside my body. It's terrifying."

Lily wrapped her arms around herself. No matter how hard she squeezed or how roughly she rubbed, she couldn't generate the heat she'd received from Elek's embrace. She'd bet that if he were holding her through the night, no witch would dare enter the room, much less climb aboard her back.

"I'll stay with you."

"Are you sure?" There was no way she could hide the eagerness and delight in her voice. Nor the smile that split her lips.

Elek crossed the threshold of the balcony to her bed. He stood staring at the mattress for a long, silent moment. "Do you need to disrobe?"

Lily wanted to say yes. Skin to skin would banish not only the witches, but any nightmares. How could her mind possibly conjure anything bad when she was being held by a dream? But she also saw the discomfort in Elek's eyes.

For her, this was about a release of tension. For

him, it would be about control. While he held Lily, Elek would also have to keep a tight leash on his beast.

She should tell him not to worry about it. She should tell him to forget about it. What she did tell him was, "I just need to take off my shoes."

Elek nodded. He sat down on the bed. His weight caused the mattress to groan. The groan wasn't an unhappy sound. It was more like a welcome sigh.

Lily kicked off her shoes. She rounded the bed to the other side. She perched herself gingerly at the center of the mattress. Then she kicked up her legs and lay down.

Elek reposed next to her. He kicked off his shoes as well. His wings had retreated. The scales had smoothed out into golden skin. They lay side by side, but there was a gulf between them.

"Elek?"

"Yes, Lily?"

"It works when we're touching. If I can feel your flesh. It helps negate the spasms."

It was a shameless bid to get at his warmth. But it was also true. When Rose shook the mattress, the move didn't release Lily from her prison. It was only when she placed her hands on Lily.

Elek slid his arm across the mattress. It brushed

Lily's skin. A slight gasp escaped her at his heated touch. Lily was sure she heard him gasp, too. Or she thought she had, because within moments, Lily was asleep. And just as she predicted, she slept through the night without any enchanted visitors.

# CHAPTER ELEVEN

lek tossed the red herbs into the pot along with the crushed blue flowers. He was going for the flavor profile of sweet and spicy. Most things this past week had that flavor profile and he ignored anyone who said anything against the combination.

The first night he'd held Lily in his arms had been sweet agony. Every time she'd shifted in her sleep, he'd been knocked in the nose by the sweet floral scent of her hair. Every time she'd reached for him, her fingertips or palms coming flush with his flesh, he'd felt certain that the sheets would combust.

Luckily, no bedclothes were harmed during Elek and Lily's sleepovers. No fair maidens either. Elek's beast had behaved each night he'd gathered Lily into his arms to help keep her internal monsters at bay. And it had worked.

Lily hadn't had a single episode of a witch visitor. Or an episode of sleep paralysis. Corun had explained the phenomenon to Elek.

There was no evil presence lurking in the shadows, waiting to attack Lily. There were no psychiatric wounds from Lily's past, as she'd suspected. It all came down to stress.

Lily had spent much of her life in a stressful home and work environment. Now that that was all in the past, and she had not a care in the world and food in her belly, she was sleeping soundly through the night.

It was likely unnecessary for Elek to hold her each night. He neglected to relay that bit of information to her. She seemed to enjoy his company, but more importantly, the nightly visits to her bed kept his dragon at bay. Meaning it was what was best for each party involved.

Lily got her rest. The dragon got to play mate, albeit in a chaste way. And Elek maintained his peace of mind. All was well.

"You can't serve a dish of meat to fairies," said Ilia. This was said with a lick of his chops. The jade-eyed dragon was clearly hoping for a larger portion of the glazed raptor.

"King Gyges is a carnivore," said Elek, lowering the flame to let the meat rest. "His ancestors were one of Her incarnations of the Venus Flytrap."

Ilia sucked his teeth at that bit of information, which announced he would be getting a normal portion tonight.

The dragons were hosting not only the Fairy King for dinner but also the heads of the three shifter families. It was all part of Kimber's Accords which had brought the first spate of peace to the Veil in centuries. Before the Accords, lions, wolves, bears and dragons had fought for any human female sacrifice presented through the cracks of the two worlds by gem-hungry human males. Even when one particular species won the right to claim a sacrifice, there could still be in-fighting amongst their own kind. That was how all the other dragon weyrs had died out.

Elek placed the cloche over the glazed raptor and handed it to Ilia with a meaningful look. His brother smirked, but kept his hands under the serving tray without lifting the lid as they brought the food out to the dining room.

The girls had done up the great hall well. The

nice china was laid out over delicate white lace. Hundreds of candles lit the room instead of the bulbed chandelier.

Kimber held Cardi high in his arms as she struck a match and lit a few candles to the side of the room. Poppy sat at the door nearest the restroom. Beryl hovered over her, his gaze lifting from her belly to her face and back. Lily stood with her sister at the far side of the room. She wore a shimmering gown that hugged each and every one of her curves.

The sight made Elek trip as he crossed the threshold. Luckily, Elek was an agile dragon and the dish only teetered. When Lily caught him staring, she offered him a shy smile. That smile was brighter than the fairy dust of her dress.

Another thing that dusted her was his scent. Sleeping together each night covered Lily from head to toe in the musk of his dragon. His claiming mark on her neck made it visible that she was his, even if his beast hadn't claimed her in the ancient ways. So when Konan, the elder of wolves, was the first to arrive with his flaring nostrils, Elek relaxed back in his seat with the knowledge that Lily was safe from the man's sniffing beast.

The bear elder Turin followed after the wolf. He gave Kimber a hearty handshake and Cardi a big bear-hug. Next to arrive was Leona, the matriarch of the lions. She eyed the head of the table, but contented herself with the seat to Kimber's right, which had been reserved for Cardi. Cardi kissed Leona on her cheek and sat in Kimber's lap as she talked the lioness's ear off until the guest of honor showed up.

Gyges arrived more than fashionably late, decked out in enough fashion to hurt Elek's eyes. The purple fairy was dressed in a loud shade of zebra print with a furry mane of pink. Sparkling gloves covered his hands and a jewel-tipped cane crashed against the floor with each step.

Elek took his seat at the far end of the table from the loud fairy. He sat across from Lily, who eyed the spectacle with quiet wonder. Elek took a moment to be sure it was wonder that held her breath and not overwhelm. The last thing he wanted was for Lily to go frozen in a catatonic state like she had the last time this many male shifters were in the room.

This time, none of the males were looking at her with carnal intent. Not when the scent of Elek coated her skin and his mark was on her neck.

"Are you planning new games?" asked Kimber after the main dishes were cleared away and dessert was being served.

Gyges poked at the fudge-brownie cookie on his plate as though it were a microwaved dinner. The fairy had picked at his food all evening. If his intention was to cause offense, Elek took none. Not when Lily had asked for seconds of each dish served.

"My games are on hiatus for the time being," said Gyges. "Those infernal Knights are making things difficult for any fun to be had these days."

The Knights of Caerleon were the protectors of witches back on the other side of the Veil. Just as shifters and fairies weren't supposed to cross the Veil into the human world, the knights and witches weren't supposed to cross to this side, either. Gyges had flaunted that rule for centuries until he'd been recently caught and shut down by the Knights.

Before that, he'd run elaborate games in such places as the Roman Colosseum, the temples of Alexandria, Egypt, and the ancient Mayan ball courts in Palenque. The games pitted humans against magical creatures for sport. The prizes were life-changing, but the cost was often death.

"My daughter recently wed one of them." Gyges sniffed, pushing his dessert plate away.

"A human?" asked Kimber.

"Yes, and she bred with one of those low creatures, a knight at that, if you can believe it."

"A human and a fae?" said Kimber. "Is that even possible?"

From his perch outside the kitchen window where he'd been gnawing on the bones of the raptor, Rhyol perked up. The dragon often made itself scarce when guests were over. Since he could no longer shift back into his human form, Rhyol saw no reason to play nice with anyone outside of his family.

"Apparently, it is," Gyges was saying. "Now I'll have a half-breed sprouting up in my pristine family line."

Gyge's attention turned to Poppy and her increasing belly. "Looks like your weyr continues to weaken with halflings."

Beryl bristled. Poppy snagged her mate's hand and rested it on her belly. Beryl's shoulders relaxed, but he didn't take his eyes off the purple fairy across the table.

Gyge's attention next turned to Lily. "I see you have another sacrifice up for offer."

All the air was sucked out of the room with that statement. The sounds of forks scraping against china came to a dead halt. Loud gulps permeated the atmosphere as goblets were snatched from lips so that predatory noses could sniff the air.

"She's Elek's mate," said Kimber, the picture of calm.

Gyges tsked and shook his head. "He may have suckled the sap, but she has not been plucked."

Lily's face went red. The blush was the only thing moving across her features. She didn't blink. She didn't breathe. She didn't even flinch. Elek sat across from her, watching the signs of a catatonic state tug at her being.

"Is this true?" asked Konan, his wolfish whiskers twitching as though he could scent out just how far Elek's and Lily's relationship went. "If the woman is untouched, she is fair game."

Inside his mind, Elek's dragon roared. Its claws came out, ripping at Elek's gut to get out. It took every bit of willpower Elek had to keep the beast from bursting out of his skin and causing maximum damage, the type of damage that had taken down weyrs.

"Touch my sister and I'll rip your cock off," said Rose, a butter knife in her hand as she faced off against males who, even when not in their shifted forms, towered over her and were twice as broad.

Lily remained still and mute. Her eyes lifted to Elek. He could hear her pleading with him, but he was powerless to go to her. If he moved even a fraction of an inch, the dragon would get free and all hell would break loose.

"They are the rules," said Leona, her lion's eyes glowing with possession of what she might bring home for her cubs.

"You're basically saying that if Elek doesn't fuck her right now, you have the right to take her?" said Rose. "Well, fuck that, and fuck you, too."

"It's the rule." That was said quietly from the bear's large mouth.

Turin looked to Kimber. Kimber sat tense with his hands clenched around a fork. Gyges sipped his tea and grinned. Seemed he'd found a game he could play tonight. One that would reap more carnage than any in the past, unless it was handled deftly. Luckily, Elek's oldest brother excelled at deft.

"They can't have her, Kimby," said Cardi. "Tell them."

Kimber looked at Elek, then Lily, and then back again. "It's the rule," he said finally.

# CHAPTER TWELVE

Lily sat frozen in the high-backed chair. She felt the claws running down her back, looking for the perfect vertebrae in which to dig into her spine. The witch was shameless tonight, making her presence known in a room full of people while Lily was wide awake.

This had happened before. Many times when she would go on modeling castings. The men, and even some of the women, would look her up and down, pick over the flaws of her body, determine her worth and her value. All the while, Lily could only stand there, mute, trying to stand statuesque and tall, look as thin as possible, emulate a blank slate upon which they would paint. It was the same feeling as when she was asleep and unable to move her limbs when the witch claimed her. She'd thought those days were over for her, but here in the castle where she'd believed she was safe, it was happening again.

"Last week she looked too frail," said the lioness. "But now that you've fattened her up, she'll be perfect for one of my cubs."

"The red hair is unfortunate as wolves can't perceive that color well, but she would do for my pack."

"Every time a sacrifice has come through the Veil these last decades, we bears have been hibernating. At this point, my clan will take what we can get."

This was a nightmare. A living, breathing nightmare while she was wide awake. Wide awake and surrounded by people. Surrounded by people, yet the one who had promised to protect her sat just as silent and immobile as her.

Elek's hands were clenched into tight fists, so tight that a trickle of blood leaked from his palms. His teeth were gritted so hard that Lily worried she might hear the grinding if it weren't for the arguing all around them. But it was his eyes that made her heart stop.

There was a bright, golden glow emitting from Elek's eyes. It made Lily think of the film they watched last week, *The Last Dragon.* But it didn't look like Elek was reaching the next level and finding the master within. As the golden glow shimmered over his body, it looked like he was in the fight of his life to master the beast within.

Lily raised a hand to him. She didn't want Elek and his beast to fight. What if the beast won, and she lost Elek forever? What if Elek won and a part of him died? All because she couldn't stand up for herself.

"Stop."

The single word was spoken softly, but the command was loud enough to bring silence down in the dining room.

Lily was so caught up in the prickles at her spine that she didn't immediately realize that the word had come from her. Her hand was raised in the midst of her paralysis. Not only that, but she was standing.

She had stood up for herself.

All eyes were on her now. In awe? In judgement? She didn't give any of them consideration, because the only pair of eyes she cared about still glowed in an intense battle.

Elek's nostrils flared. His chest heaved up and

down. But he did not speak. It looked like he could not.

Lily couldn't abide seeing him this way. She would not be the cause of another soul suffering the way she had for all of her life. Especially not this man who had given her everything of himself that he could and had asked nothing in return.

"Elek," she said. "Elek, I release you from our bond."

The light in his eyes died out. His chest caved in and his shoulders slumped. He breathed heavy, shallow, panting breaths that burned the lace of the tablecloth. Lily had to assume that since he hadn't shifted, the man had won the battle.

"She's denied the dragon's claim," said the lioness. "That means she's fair game."

Lily felt every unattached male's gaze bore into her. She felt the heat from their glowing eyes. She heard a chorus of sharp *clings* as their claws unsheathed.

Rose kicked her chair back and came to Lily's side. "None of you are taking my sister."

"It's the rules," snarled the wolf.

"The rules suck," said Cardi. "This is why women don't want to come here. You keep fighting over them. We're liberated twentieth-century women in here."

"Twenty-first century," said Chryssie.

"What?" said Cardi. "Oh, right."

"Still, the new rules say she gets to choose, remember," said Chryssie. "If Lily has changed her mind about Elek, fine. But she gets to choose how she lives her life and who she wants to live it with."

Kimber held up a finger. "That's not exactly—"

Cardi whipped her head around to glare at her mate. "If you want access to your women, then you'll follow our rules. You'll all follow our rules. We're done with being told what to do."

"You didn't complain last—"

"Shush."

The hard-as-ice dragon leader shut his trap. So, too, did every other mated dragon around the table. The other shifters hadn't taken their gazes off Lily, but they held to their seats. Meanwhile, the fairy king slurped down a second cup of tea with a smirk on his too-handsome face.

"Either back us," said Cardi. "Or see the back of us."

That got a smile out of Kimber.

"Shut up. You know what I mean."

Kimber turned his attention to Lily. "Tell us what you want, Lily?"

What did she want? All her life, Lily had tried to be what others wanted. No one had ever asked her that question.

No. That wasn't true. One man had.

Lily looked across the table…but that man was gone.

All eyes were on her again. She waited for the paralysis to return, but the witch had fled out the window on her broomstick. With how light her shoulders felt and how straight she stood, Lily doubted she would ever see the hag again.

Lily wasn't entirely sure what she wanted, but she knew what she didn't want. She didn't want to be the one put on display. She didn't want to be the one to be judged. If she was going to need a mate to stay here, she was going to do the choosing, and they were going to play *her* game, by *her* rules.

## CHAPTER THIRTEEN

He knew he'd made the wrong decision the moment he left the room. Elek just wasn't sure who the decision was wrong for. Him? Or Lily?

The beast had been pacing the insides of his belly since the moment the first shifter had walked into the castle. Its claws had gotten into Elek's chest cavity when Gyges had made his proclamation. Both man and beast had wanted nothing more than to burn the flowery man to a crisp and sprinkle him on a soufflé. Elek's dragon had nearly torn through his skin when every shifter's hackles went up at the possibility of claiming Lily.

*His Lily.*

He stood outside the castle now—just below

Lily's bedroom window—as he watched the last of the shifters leave the castle. Leona was the final guest to leave, sniffing around the interior as though she was measuring the drapes to make a move on the castle as well as Lily.

*His Lily.*

*His Lily no more.*

Within his gut, Elek could no longer feel the dragon. When Lily had released him from his claim on her, the beast had let go. Not just of the battle for dominance inside his body, the dragon had let go of its will.

Elek had won. He'd won the battle he'd been fighting since that night he'd accidentally harmed his mother and she'd never been the same again. He'd vanquished the monster inside. But in doing so, he'd lost the war.

All was quiet inside his head. Inside his heart. Inside his soul.

He had claimed the total peace he'd coveted for so long…and it felt awful.

*His Lily.*

*His Lily no more.*

*He'd lost Lily.*

That felt wrong down to his core. If Elek no longer had a claim to her, he would not be permitted to hold her, or touch her. To dig his nose into her hair, at the top of her spine, at the place behind her ear that was always a bit salty mixed in with her floral sweetness.

A large predator crashed down in front of him. With the dragon inside him groping for death, Elek didn't even raise his fists to defend himself. He didn't care to turn and face his foe, not when he could instead catch a glimpse of Lily from her bedroom window.

The color of topaz-blue filled Elek's vision. Rhyol snarled, but he still didn't get Elek's attention. Not until Rhyol swatted Elek on the back of his head with his massive claws.

"Ow," Elek grunted in annoyance, spitting out the tuft of dirt he'd gotten into his mouth when he'd hit the ground.

Rhyol had long since lost himself to the dragon. It was a path Elek didn't want to take. Rhyol sometimes had trouble making himself understood. The word *idiot* rang loud and clear in Elek's mind.

"I could never be the man she needs," said Elek, his head in his hands. "Not when I'm always fighting myself."

But did that mean that another male could? His dragon sat defeated in his gut. The truth was, Elek hadn't mastered his beast. Losing his mate was what had bested it. Although Elek knew he was not at his best himself. Not while carrying around the dead weight inside him.

The blue dragon breathing down his neck looked like he wanted to take a bite out of of Elek's hide. Elek held still as Rhyol's clawed hand came down upon him. Instead of pain, he heard his brother's voice in his head.

"She is your mate."

Elek felt the beast stir at his brother's statement.

"You need to claim her and stop this madness."

That was the point; the madness had stopped. The madness of his dragon warring with him. The madness Lily had been battling each night.

He'd seen her slip into a catatonic state at dinner. As he'd sat there fighting his own battle, Lily had conquered her fears. She'd slipped the grip of the immobile stupor and had stood up, claiming herself.

Warmth bloomed in his chest at the memory of that—Lily, standing up for herself.

"Hurry," Rhyol urged, looking up to Lily's window. "Or you will lose not only her, but you'll lose yourself as well."

His brother was wrong. Rhyol had lost his battle

with his dragon. But Rhyol had lost to the dragon. Elek was still a man at the end of his battle.

Rhyol shook his head. His brother had heard Elek's thoughts. Rhyol withdrew his hand from Elek's shoulder, but not before Elek caught a string of expletives detailing just what the blue dragon thought of the outcome of Elek's internal struggles.

"I should have stood by her in that dining hall and not walked away," Elek admitted. "I was wrong for that."

Rhyol snorted, but Elek was certain that in that snort were more curse words.

The light was still on in Lily's bedroom. He could hear the chatter of the other women in there with her. He was certain he would get an earful from the women when he made his appearance, but it was a punishment he would take to offer Lily an apology. With a roll of his shoulders, Elek called to his wings.

Nothing happened.

He cracked his neck from side-to-side, releasing the pressure in the bones. He windmilled first one, and then the other arm. Then he called to his wings again.

Nothing.

Elek looked at his brother. "Can you give me a lift?"

Rhyol grabbed him by the scruff of the neck. His brother's handling wasn't the most gentle, but it got the job done. Rhyol dropped Elek on Lily's balcony and then flew off into the night.

When Elek knocked on the balcony door, it was Cardi who answered. She shut the curtains behind her and pulled the door closed. Crossing her arms over her chest, she lifted a brow at Elek.

"Can I speak to her?" he asked.

"She doesn't want to see you."

There was a hushed silence in the room beyond. Elek easily picked out Lily's breath. He'd been listening to her even breathing for the past week as she'd slept in his arms. He hated that he would have to give that up, but if it came at the cost of Lily coming into her own power, it was a price he'd pay.

"I can understand if she is angry with me. I hope I can make my apologies in the morning."

"The Sacrifice, Lily Bishop, will not be seeing any males aiming to claim her before the Games," Cardi said with a roll of her neck.

"Games?"

Cardi stepped back inside, slamming the door behind her. Only to reappear a moment later. "She wants you to have this."

A cold piece of metal was shoved onto his chest

before Cardi disappeared inside, shutting the curtains firmly behind her. But not before Elek caught the barest of glimpses of Lily.

She looked tired and a little frightened. More than anything, he wanted to go to her, to wrap her up in his arms, and keep all the monsters—real or imagined—away. But he was shut out.

He looked down at what she'd given him. The object looked like a talisman, similar to the charm Bruce Leeroy's teacher had given him when he'd begun his quest for the Golden Glow. It was a quest that had ultimately led to Leroy finding mastery within himself.

# CHAPTER FOURTEEN

Lily sat back on the couch. Though it was more of a chaise lounge—the kind she'd seen Elizabeth Taylor languish on in her role as Cleopatra.

There were even jewels along the armrest. Bright orange gems of amber that shone at her in the late morning sunlight. They twinkled up at her, warming the underside of her chin with their glow —much like Elek's breath had done when he'd held her as she'd pretended to sleep all last week.

Each night, Lily had fought sleep to bask in Elek's care. Even when sleep had inevitably won the battle, she'd still sensed him all around her, like a guardian angel, protecting her as she rested.

Her guardian angel hadn't been on duty last night. He wasn't here this morning. He was nowhere in sight.

Lily's back went stiff against the couch. Or lounge. Or chaise. Or whatever.

The piece of furniture wasn't uncomfortable. There were cushions and pillows—so many pillows. It was the position she was in that was so unfamiliar to her.

Her back had been pressed up against many casting couches with powerful men looming over her. She realized now that their power had only come from the fealty she'd given them. None had had strength. Few had had any muscle not surgically designed and attached to their flesh. None could breathe fire, or fly, or shift their shapes.

All the males coming into the gates could do that. Men who could shift into beasts capable of crushing any one of the humans who had made Lily feel so small not too long ago. But now it was Lily on the couch. It was *her* directing this call. It was *she* who held all the power as these men came to pledge their loyalty to her.

For the first time in her life, Lily felt powerful.

"Microphone check. One, two, one two," Cardi

called into the mic. She then began popping her lips and making belching and wheezing sounds. "It's Cardi in the house. We gonna blow the roof off this mother."

"We're not inside, Cardi," said Poppy. "There's no roof to blow anywhere."

Poppy sat with her feet up on another couch. The emerald-green sofa-cushions were so soft that her butt sank right in and made her belly look like it was floating.

Chryssie came up from the side of the raised platform on which Lily's chaise rested. She piled two more pillows onto the chaise lounge; one behind Lily's head and the other under her feet. "You comfortable, sis?"

For a while last night, Lily had been heartbroken that she had lost Elek. Then she'd been flanked by four of the strongest, most loving, most fun women she'd ever met. She may have lost a mate, but she'd gained three new sisters.

"I'm good. Thanks, Chryssie."

Chryssie bussed the side of Lily's temple, then turned to deal with the males milling around the grounds of the castle. As part of the deal the women had struck to run the Mating Games themselves, the dragons hung back. But it was impossible not to feel the ice of diamonds, the cut of rubies, the darkness of jade, and the sharp blade of emerald—the dragon shifter eyes staring back at them.

The other shifters certainly felt it, too. They each fidgeted as they came to the end of the raised stage and listened to Chryssie's instructions. This was the women's show, and all the men would get in line.

"You ready for this?" Rose sat on the arm of the chaise.

Was Lily ready for this?

Chryssie gave a rolled tapestry a kick. The red carpet unfolded down a long runway, ending in a *flap-flap* at the booted feet of the contenders. The males looked at the length of the long rug in confusion.

"Yes." Lily grinned. "I'm ready."

She and the other women had spent all night devising the games that the men would have to play in order to be considered for a chance to mate Lily. This was the first of three tasks. It was a gift-giving.

This task was Cardi's idea. Her icon Madonna had proven in the *Material Girl* music video that a girl could tell a lot about a man by what he valued and was willing to share. Though it had been the movie-producer—who'd stalked her through half the video and then pretended he was poor by giving her wilting daisies and carting her off in a beat-up pickup truck—who had won Madge's affections. Rose had tried to point out the hypocrisy, but both Poppy and Chryssie had shaken their heads and shushed her.

"All righty, boys," Cardi's voice was husky on the microphone. "You wanna shoot your shot?"

Every male gathered cocked his head like a dog, sensing there was a treat to be had but unsure if punishment was also on the menu. In the distance, there was a growl that could only belong to Kimber.

"We live in a material world," Cardi went on, oblivious to her double entendre. "So show this material girl what you have to offer."

The first contestant stepped up. It was the lion Izem. The man reminded Lily of a cleaned-up James Dean with his leather jacket and his golden hair in a perfectly waved coif. He strode down the carpet, the picture of confidence. At the end of the walkway, he went to one knee and presented Lily with a hair brush.

It would've been a nice gesture…if it hadn't had strands of golden hair in the bristles. Strands that were the exact shade of his.

The second contestant was a bear—Turin, from

the dinner party the other night. He wore a white t-shirt that was bursting at the seams trying to hold his muscles in. Turin presented Lily with the largest salmon she'd ever seen.

Lily's mouth watered at the delicious-looking fish. She couldn't wait to take it to the kitchen and see what spices Elek would add to it.

Elek…

Lily gave her head a shake. She would not think of Elek. When she accepted the claim of one of these males—which she would inevitably have to do—she would no longer live in the castle. She wouldn't see her new sisters every day, much less the amber-eyed dragon.

Lily sat graciously, body poised and smile in place, just as she'd been taught from all her years modeling. She nodded at each gift, not giving any of the shifters a clue as to which way she was leaning in the games.

There was a lull in the games as the wolf shifter, Konan, prepared his gift. The sun was at its highest peak in the sky. Lily was getting tired. She was thirsty and her stomach showed signs of an impending tantrum if she didn't feed it soon.

"I made this for you."

A dish of sweets appeared below Lily's nose.

Alongside the treats was a glass of what looked and smelled like lemonade, but with orange slices in it that made the liquid more amber in color.

Elek stood at the side of the chaise. There were dark circles under his eyes and his skin was pallid, no longer its rich amber tan.

"No cuts, E," Cardi called from the stage. "Sign in and get to the back of the line of you're competing."

"I'm not competing," he said, his gaze on Lily. "We're usually eating lunch with Mom at this time, and I thought you'd be hungry."

"Don't let him worm his way back into your panties without a fight," said Cardi.

"I was never in her panties."

There was a chorus of gasps, chuckles, and snorts from the peanut gallery surrounding the runway and back in the shadows of the castle.

"My intention is to earn back your friendship and your trust."

It was no longer Lily's stomach threatening a tantrum. Her heart skipped not one, but two beats.

"I've conquered my dragon," said Elek, the pallor in his face even more pronounced as his lips spread into a strained smile. "I'm proud that you've conquered your demons, too."

Whenever Lily had looked into Elek's eyes, she'd

always seen an amber light shining back at her. It was gone now. Like the bulb had gone dead.

"Excuse me," called the next contestant. "Are we having a competition here? Or a tea party?"

Elek bowed his head to Lily and took a step back. Lily fought the urge to reach for him. The dimness in his gaze worried her. But her attention was drawn back to the game at hand.

Konan, the wolf shifter from last night, started his strut down the runway. His hands were empty. The coat he wore was long. Every woman present collectively cringed and leaned back as he reached for the buttons of his coat.

"I present to you what every woman wants."

Konan reached down and flung his coat opened with both hands. His present was exactly what they'd all expected it to be. Instead of gasping or screeching in outrage, each woman's head canted to the side.

"Not bad," said Rose. "My mate's is bigger."

"Not as big as Kimby's."

"Corun's is seriously impressive. I have to soak every morning."

"You see what Beryl's did to me on the first go?"

Lily looked off to the side where Elek had

retreated. She'd felt his unveiling against her back each morning when she woke up. What Konan was working with likely paled in comparison. But she would never know for sure.

# CHAPTER FIFTEEN

Elek watched the feathers as they flew up in the air. There were seven of them, each a hue featured in a rainbow. The orange one sailed down and landed on his nose. He huffed out a breath to dislodge the plume, and it was extinguished in a puff of smoke.

It hadn't been Elek's fire. At his side, Corun pressed his lips together. His smirk said he was satisfied that his fire had laid waste to at least one piece of costuming in here.

The competing shifters were all arranged just inside the dragon mines as they prepared for the next bout of obstacles in Lily's mating games.

"Exactly what is this fashion show accomplishing?" asked Turin as he slung a golden sash with his name etched on it over his shoulder.

"To make sure we look good beside her," said Leander, securing a sash with his own name over his outfit. "It will show compatibility of style."

"It's so she can get a good look at our packages." Konan placed his sash over his bare chest. The rest of his outfit consisted only of gray sweatpants.

"Does this outfit make my butt look big?" Izem turned in the mirror of diamonds to look at his ass, then got caught admiring himself.

Kimber huffed out a puff of smoke as he kept a watchful eye on each of the shifters gazing at their reflections in the gems he'd mined in this cave. Beryl had his back to his emeralds and Ilia minded the jade gems he'd been mining all his life. Rhyol paced back and forth, his wings spread in front of the sparkling blue pile of topaz he'd dug up with his bare claws.

Elek cast a glance at his horde of amber gemstones. He'd been neglecting his mining duties the last week that he'd been caring for Lily. Looking at the collection now, his gaze zeroed in on a particular stone. The glow of the stone was more golden than orange, reflecting the color of Lily's skin.

Her flesh had looked sallow when she'd first

arrived, her body thin, her cheeks gaunt. Within days of being here and eating everything he'd set before her, Lily had stood taller. Her curves had filled out. Her skin had begun to glow with a healthy radiance.

Elek picked up the stone. It was warm in his hands. The warmth reminded him of the feel of her skin when he'd held her close each night.

"Tell me, Elek. Does the maid like flowers or glitter?" Turin held up a shirt with pale flowers and another with sparkles.

"Why are you asking him?" said Konan. "He couldn't keep hold of her. Trust me when I tell you, when I sink my claws into that bony flesh, she will be begging for me to not let go."

Corun was in front of Elek before Elek had realized he'd moved. His teeth were bared, his fists clenched, and his eyes saw red. The beast within was alive, awake, and out for blood.

"Easy, Elek," said Corun.

It wasn't Elek that his brother needed to cool. It was the dragon inside him. Except…a glance inside himself showed the dragon still lying on his back, eyes closed, chest barely moving.

"I thought you didn't want to mate?" said Leander.

Elek waited for the dragon to rear its head at the comment. To exhale a furious fire at the notion of not wanting Lily. The beast didn't lift a claw or utter a breath.

Elek took a deep breath. The oxygen expanded his chest, but did not rouse the fire inside of him. He opened his mouth to speak, but no words came out. He took another breath and tried again.

"I want what is best for Lily. She has had a rough time in life. She does not deserve any more hardship. If I find that one of you gives her a moment of grief, you will be dealing with my beast."

Every male in the room shuffled his feet, none raised their eyes or their voice. Few had actually encountered Elek's dragon, but all had heard of the size and power of his beast. None knew that his threat was a bluff.

Feeling that his point had been made, Elek left the mines. He staggered when he came face-to-face with the setting sun. It felt as though it had taken every last ounce of his energy to make it from there to here.

"Elek."

Elek stopped walking at the sound of his brother's voice, but he didn't turn. He didn't need for Corun to tell him that something was wrong.

"You don't look good," said Corun as he rounded on him.

The scientist in the family peered at Elek with a discerning gaze. Elek felt poked and prodded in every place his brother's gaze landed on his person.

"I'm at peace," Elek said. "I've conquered my dragon."

"Have you, now?"

"It hasn't stirred in a full day."

Corun didn't look impressed at Elek's feat. Nothing but concern laced his ruby-colored eyes.

Searching for strength, Elek pressed the talisman Lily had given him into his palm. Of course, he knew there was no power in the object. What it carried was Lily's scent. She must have worn it close to her body before giving it to him. It was her scent that gave him strength. As long as she was hearty and hale, Elek would retain his peace.

"It doesn't work that way."

Elek lifted his gaze to his brother.

"Man and beast must coexist," Corun went on to explain. "We are born together and must learn to live together if we are to thrive."

"For years, you've been searching for a way to suppress the beast within."

Corun shook his head. "That theory was proven

wrong when I met Chryssie. It was proven wrong for each of us who met our mate. It's not dominance that sets us free, it's balance."

Elek pressed his lips together. He looked off towards the platform. The girls had strung fairy lights along the runway in preparation for the show. The sound of Lily's laughter carried to him on the slight breeze. A shiver ran over Elek's shoulders.

"You're cold?" said Corun. "Dragon's don't get cold."

Elek didn't respond. He simply gazed at Lily. He would be happy to stand at a distance and gaze at her for the rest of his days. Behind him, the other shifters began to file out of the mines and head towards the red carpet of the runway.

Soon, Lily would select one of them to hold her close at night. One of those males would offer to feed her from his hands. One of them would sheath himself inside her sweet and spicy flesh.

Once again, Elek's eyes glazed over in red. The fire of anger burned somewhere within him, but on the outside he shivered again.

"If your dragon is silent, then you have no fire," said Kimber. "If you have no fire, you cannot warm yourself and you will not find balance as a man."

"I did not ask you for a fortune-cookie lecture, brother."

"I'm trying to save your life."

"Rhyol lost himself to the dragon," said Elek. "If I have lost, at least I retain my manhood."

"Rhyol made the choice to retreat, but he's still in there. Meanwhile, the dragon becomes more feral every day. Soon, there will come a day when we will no longer be able to reason with him. If you and your dragon can't find a way to live together, you will become a shell of your former self, never knowing true peace again."

# CHAPTER SIXTEEN

Right Said Fred's *I'm Too Sexy* blasted across the speakers as the next shifter did an about-face and walked to the opposite end of the runway. Lily had to hand it to the guys. So far they'd walked the runway with poise. Each shifter strode with confidence, his broad shoulders back, his head high as his muscled chest led the charge down the red carpet.

"Guess he's too sexy for his shirt," Cardi said as Konan strode down the runway.

The wolf shifter's chest was bare, save for the sash across his torso. Konan wore a pair of grey sweatpants that left nothing to the imagination. At least this time he'd worn pants. His walk, just like his personality, was far too aggressive for Lily. He stomped down the runway as though he was prowling for a bunny in the clearing.

"No way he's disco dancing," said Chryssie as Izem took to the runway next.

The lion shifter wore a white suit with large lapels over a black-collared shirt, *a la* John Travolta in *Saturday Night Fever.* Sure enough, when he got to the end of the runway, he struck the trademark pose of the franchise, one hand in the air, finger pointing to the sky.

"I like it," said Cardi, rolling her arms and alternately pointing to the sky along with Izem. "He's got style and rhythm."

"He's too pretty," said Rose. "We knew men like him in the modeling industry, didn't we, Lils?"

Lily wasn't listening to the women. She wasn't paying that much attention to the show either. Her gaze kept drifting off to the castle.

She'd seen Elek leave the mines and head for the castle before the show started. He'd glanced her way, and he'd looked…troubled. Was he having second thoughts about his claim on her?

If he was, then he should be out here fighting for her hand like the others. But he wasn't. He'd disappeared inside the castle and she'd seen the kitchen lights go on.

There was also a waft on the cool evening breeze of something sweet and savory coming from that direction. Lily's stomach threatened to pitch a tantrum. It had been a few hours since she'd appeased it. Maybe she could take a break and grab a bite?

"Leander is still my favorite," said Poppy.

"Oh, really?" Chryssie cocked her head to the side thoughtfully. "I like Turin for Lily. Big and brawny has always done it for me."

"Leander's big and broody," said Cardi. "What would they have to talk about? I've been to the bears' caves. The lighting is awful. You'd never get your makeup on right."

"Lil?" said Rose. "Lily, what do you think?"

Lily blinked a few times before focusing on the women around her. The last man had finished his stroll down the catwalk. They all stood at the edge, waiting for her attention. Lily opened her mouth, but her stomach growled, making its desires heard the length of the red carpet.

For years, Lily had pushed her own desires down —so far down that she no longer knew what they were. That wasn't true today.

Today, she didn't want to make any decisions about her future. Today, she just wanted to have whatever Elek was cooking in the kitchen. Or rather, her stomach did. And so that's what she would have.

"Thank you all for coming and participating in the first two rounds of the mating games," she said. "You've given me a lot to think about. I look forward to seeing you tomorrow for the last round."

And with that, Lily stepped down from the dais. Surprisingly, none of the girls followed her into the castle. She heard them all whispering and giggling behind her, but the sounds from her stomach were much louder, and she paid them more heed.

Lily didn't much remember the walk to the kitchen. If anyone had asked how she'd gotten there so fast, she would've told them she'd flown. Just like in the cartoon when tendrils of the aroma of a good-smelling dish lifted the character up by the nose and levitated them to the dish. At the end of that journey, the cartoon character was always left in some sort of peril. When Lily walked into the door of the kitchen she was met with…nothing.

Nothing except food. Elek was not there.

The fire in the hearth was cool. It looked as though it hadn't been lit since yesterday. Covered dishes were set on the modern-looking stove. It was clear when she went closer that he had used the burners there, which was odd. Elek said he liked controlling the cooking fire with his own flame.

Lily knew which dish was meant to be hers. It was set out on the amber-colored plate Elek often handed her. She lifted the cloche and a waft of enticing scents smacked her in the nose. What made her heart skip was the heart-shaped gem left on the tray.

Lily stood at the counter and ate each morsel one by one. Her gaze flicked from the clock, then to the door. As the minute hand ticked by and circled back around to the hour hand, the plate cleared. Nobody came into the kitchen.

Gathering up the gem and holding it close to her chest, Lily left the kitchen and climbed the stairs to her room. The moon was high in the sky and the lights inside the castle were low.

Though she knew nothing in the castle would hurt her, she still was hesitant to be out of her room alone late at night. There were all manner of sounds, creaks, and yawns, of the old structure. Not to mention the moans and groans coming from behind bedroom doors.

When she reached her room, she climbed onto

the bed and began a staring contest with the ceiling. She knew that sleep would elude her. She was tired, but she was also keyed up. She had men vying for her, each of them wanting to impress *her*, and not the other way around. The problem was, Lily didn't feel a spark for any of them.

The only one who got any sort of reaction from her was Leander. But she got more friend-vibes from the lion than anything. She had enough friends. She was wasting time with this game.

Elek was the only one who did it for her. Her body only responded to him. She couldn't imagine allowing another male to touch her, bite her, or anything else her. Not when Elek's mark still throbbed at her neck.

While she still ached for him, he finally seemed to have achieved the calm he'd craved his whole life. It appeared his beast was under control, now that there was no longer a mate enticing it. Meanwhile, Lily, who had never had a libido, had a raging need to have Elek's dragon claim her in every nook and cranny of her body.

Thoughts of Elek floated through her head. She tried to replace those thoughts with the faces of the other shifters. It wasn't working. Her body remained hot and bothered as she fought to change her mind. When she tried to move, she found that she could not. With her mind and body at odds, the old witch had climbed onto her back and attacked.

# CHAPTER SEVENTEEN

He wasn't sure how the beast knew she was in danger, but it knew. It roared to life inside Elek's gut, seizing his will and snatching control of his entire being. Elek was so tired, so cold, so weary, that he let it.

He couldn't have stopped the dragon if he'd tried. Elek had no cause to try. Not when Lily needed him.

All was quiet in the castle. His brothers and their mates had gone to bed after their usual bouts of vociferous bedsport. The other shifters had long since returned to their dens and caves for the night to prepare for the final day of games to claim Lily's hand. Elek was the one Lily called out to in her time of distress.

That knowledge made his feet go faster. It brought his wings from his back. His heel struck the ground one moment and the next he was airborne.

Up he flew until he was at her bedroom door. He didn't bother knocking. All sense of manners and decorum had left his mind now that the dragon was in charge. The beast burst into the room and roared at the sight before him.

Lily lay on the bed. Her body was tense, as though a war were being raged beneath her skin. Her eyes were wide and filled with terror.

The dragon shoved through the doorway, but it did not get far. With his wings extended, his large body would not fit.

Elek was beside himself, inside himself. Terror had been the last expression on his mother's face before the light had gone out in her eyes. That terror had been directed at him.

With that memory at the forefront of his mind, Elek was no help to his beast. The dragon retracted his wings, pulling them tight to his back. Finally, it managed to slip inside the door.

On the bed, Lily's chest worked in slow, rhythmic breathing. Her pinky finger twitched, then her pinky toe. She was wrestling back control from the paralysis that had tried to claim her.

The dragon dove onto the bed, scooping her up and against his chest with its claws. Like a light switch coming on, the spell was broken. Lily arched her back. She gasped and then clung to him.

Carefully, gently, the dragon held onto her. His claws were out, but the sharp nails glided up and down Lily's back in slow, soothing motions. His fangs were exposed as the beast slowed its breathing to match hers. There was a fire raging in his belly, but not a single puff of smoke escaped to singe any part of her, or the contents of the room.

In that moment, Elek was certain of one thing in this life. His dragon would never harm Lily. It would rather die than be the cause of any of her pain. Yet if she showed any signs of distress, it would move heaven and hell, and even Elek himself, to get to her.

"Don't let me go."

He hadn't imagined her words. Her voice was in his head. It rang clear, as if she had shouted her desires to his face.

"I want you to stay with me."

Lily curled her body into his lap. She dug her fingers into his robes and tucked her toes in just behind his knee. Looking down at his Lily's bare feet felt like the most intimate thing in his life.

With her increasing belly, Poppy walked around

the castle with bare feet every day. Cardi and Chryssie always sat on his mother's bed without their shoes. However, Elek had never once fixated on any of their bare toes. He couldn't take his eyes off Lily's pink toes.

"I don't want any of them. I only want you."

Now Elek knew the dragon was hallucinating. Or projecting, at the very least. It was giving voice to its own hopes and desires.

"I know you can hear me." Lily pulled away from him.

Surprisingly, the dragon let her go. But remained near enough that both man and beast could peer down into Lily's eyes. Her orbs glistened with unshed tears.

"I know you don't want me, but…" She lifted her gaze to him. Just as quickly, she glanced away. Her shoulders hunched, her head bowing, her fingers twisting around each other.

Elek opened his mouth to fill the silence. What came out was a roar. The dragon had the reins, and it was not relinquishing them. For her part, Lily didn't flinch at the dragon's cry.

"Kimber said it was my choice who I want to mate with. I didn't get to choose you the first time. You were stuck with me."

Elek wanted to argue that point. He hadn't been stuck with her. He had come to crave her company, her smiles, her scent.

"If it's my choice, I choose you. We don't have to…"

Lily left the sentence open. In their mind, the dragon filled in every sordid detail of what he wanted to do to Lily if he got the chance. It was a good thing the beast had no command of speech or—

"I want you." The dragon's words were full of smoke and grit, but they were understandable.

"You do?"

The dragon was done talking. It wrapped its arms—Elek's arms—around Lily and pulled her close. It tilted its chin—Elek's chin—to the side to gain better access to Lily's parted lips. It pressed its mouth—Elek's mouth—to Lily's in a searing kiss that made both man and beast forget who, what, where, and when they were.

Elek had never kissed a woman before. He had no idea how the dragon knew how to accomplish the feat. Or was *he* the one nipping at Lily's bottom lip? Flicking his tongue over her upper lip? Deepening the kiss by capturing the back of her head and pulling her impossibly closer?

He knew for sure that it was Lily who tugged them down to the mattress. For sure, it was Lily who spread her thighs so that his hips came between hers, his hardening cock resting on her belly.

"Is this okay?" she asked.

"Hmmm," was the only response that came from his chest. The beast in him nudged aside the top of her dress to find its mark and lick at it.

Lily's whole body shivered at the first touch of his tongue. He wondered where else he could lick that would make her shiver with such pleasure?

He tried behind her ear. That got him another shiver. She arched her neck, giving him more access to the sensitive flesh there.

He trailed his tongue down her neck. That trail was both salty and sweet. A soft moan escaped Lily's lips, and the beast went lower.

It nosed aside the top of her shirt, exposing the curve of one breast. Lily arched her back, causing her nipple to brush against his mouth. In a heart-beat, the dragon latched onto the tight bud.

Lily's cry of pleasure drowned out Elek's moan of delight. Or was it the dragon who moaned? He could no longer tell. Did he even care?

Down his lips traveled, taking in every nuance of her flesh. The heat. The cool. The ridges of her elbows. The smoothness of her belly. The salt that had collected in her belly button. She was the most complex dish he'd ever had and he couldn't get his fill.

A scent beckoned him further south…down between her parted thighs. Elek had a brief moment of clarity. In that moment, he saw that there was no longer a leash between him and the beast. The animal in him had free rein, and it had decided exactly the path it was going to take the two of them.

# CHAPTER EIGHTEEN

*L*ily had heard of girls talking about boys making them feel the way she was feeling right now. The thought of someone down there had never appealed to her. She could barely tolerate kissing on the mouth.

Elek's mouth on hers had changed her mind. His lips had felt like they were devouring her piece by blessed piece. His tongue had made her feel like she was the sweetest dessert that he'd had to lap up every morsel of.

That same tongue had made a feast of her body. He lit fires from her ears to her breasts down into her belly. As he parted her thighs, those flames up above still burned. She was sure she'd explode the moment he—

"Ahhhhh," she screamed at the first touch of his tongue to her core. The flesh there was far more sensitive than her lips.

Lily felt every texture of Elek's tongue. The soft bumps at the center that lapped at her folds from front to back. The firm tip that flicked at her engorged bud.

Since she'd been a child, she'd known that bud could give her a good feeling if she rubbed it long enough. She'd also come to know that after that good feeling washed over her, sleep would claim her...and everything that came with it. So she'd avoided that spot for most of her life.

"Lily?"

Elek's voice was inside her head as his hands continued to roam her body, and his tongue continued to taste her.

"Lily, are you all right?"

"Yes."

Lily wasn't sure if she answered Elek in her head or out loud. She wasn't sure if she heard him speaking to her at all. Her heart was in her ears. The blood had rushed from her head to pool at that good spot between her legs. It had never felt this good when she'd touched herself, and Elek showed no signs of slowing down.

"It's so—ahhh, good. Please…please don't stop. I want…I want it."

"I want it, too."

There were two different beings touching Lily. Elek touched her mind, checking her consent. The dragon within him touched her body with wild abandon. Or was it the other way around?

She wasn't sure. She couldn't focus on anything except the rising sensations in her core. The pressure had never been this intense. She felt full, like a balloon filling far beyond its capacity. Any second now, she was going to—

"Ahhhhh," she screamed again.

Lily's thighs clapped together, but her knees did not touch. Not with Elek's face still between her thighs. His shoulders kept her legs apart so that he could continue to feast on her, lapping up every single pop of pleasure that burst from her.

She had no idea how long she shook and shivered. No idea how many times her bud pulsed and her back convulsed. She thought she might have stopped breathing at one point because her breaths were so shallow.

Elek rose up above her. His eyes glowed amber-bright. Was the beast in control now? Had it been before?

Lily didn't care. She wanted both halves of him. Together they made her feel whole. She wanted to do the same for him.

She reached up to him, her hands aimed for the buckle at his pants. When her warm flesh met the cool metal, she smiled. It was the talisman she'd given him. With trembling fingers caused by the aftershocks still rippling through her body, Lily undid Elek's belt.

He made no sound. Said no words. Only watched as she disrobed him.

Elek's skin was a dark tan, close to the color of amber. At some points, his scales shimmered over his skin as it did when his dragon was near the surface. His glowing eyes said this was another of those times.

His eyes roamed her with barely concealed hunger. Still, Lily didn't feel an ounce of fear knowing Elek was at present more animal than man. She knew the dragon would never hurt her. But she hesitated to discard the dress still wrapped across her torso. So long as it was covered, neither beast nor man could see the excess flesh she had there.

"Don't," Elek said into her mind. "You're perfect."

She had never been perfect. She had been poked

and prodded, judged and discarded, used and abused.

"Never again," Elek promised as he tore the garment from her flesh. "No one will ever hurt you again. I will protect you. We will protect you."

That last bit came out in a growl that Lily felt down into her core. Because that's where the beast had prowled to. She spread her thighs wider, welcoming all of him into her.

They both gasped as the head of his cock breached flesh. Lily had never had a man as thick as Elek. Then she remembered, Elek had never had a woman at all.

This was his first time.

Lily wished she'd made it special for him. That she'd lit candles. Or played music. Or told him how much she cared for him, that she loved him.

"This is special," he told her. "I love you."

Elek thrust into her until he was fully seated. There were no more words between them. There wasn't a need. Their bodies did the talking from that moment on.

With each roll of his hips, Elek expressed his adoration of her. With each clench of her inner walls, Lily promised him her devotion. When they climaxed together, they vowed that they were now one.

Her body was satisfied. Her mind was tired. Yet her heart was full. She'd made her choice, and he had made his. He had claimed her.

For the first time in her life, Lily fell into a deep, soundless sleep. She did not dream.

# CHAPTER NINETEEN

The beast was silent again inside Elek. It lay on its back, sprawled out and barely breathing. The reason Elek knew that it was still very much alive was because of the satisfied grin on its mug.

If he looked in a mirror, Elek was certain he would have the same satisfied grin on his own face. But leaving the bed, or rather leaving Lily, was the last thing he wanted to do. With the beast out of commission due to the sex coma it was in, Elek was back in control.

He had to admit that there were times over the last few hours where he hadn't been sure if he was fulfilling his own desires or the beast's as he moved inside Lily. Both man and beast had been insatiable.

He'd waited patiently as Lily had dozed. The first time she'd stirred in his arms, he'd nuzzled at her neck to coax her into waking. Then he'd descended back between her thighs to revisit the heaven he'd found there.

After he'd wrung as many orgasms from her as he could, she'd crawled between his legs and took his manhood into her mouth. That's when the beast had rolled over and into his coma. Elek had stayed awake and kissed his sweet Lily's lips until she'd fallen asleep again.

All through the night, sleep had eluded him. He couldn't take his eyes off the precious gem in his arms. The amber stone he'd given her sat on her desk. In the pale moonlight, it matched the color of Lily's flushed skin after their lovemaking.

Elek watched his claws on her flesh. The black nails dug into Lily's skin. When she had first come here, she'd been pale. Now she had a healthy, golden tan. The black of his nails against the honey of her skin made his belly grumble and his mouth water.

He tried to retract the nails. But, even in its slumber, the dragon would not release its hold on her. Elek could feel his wings moving against his spine, aching to get out. To unfold. To spread around Lily to protect her.

"Are you going to fly away from me again?"

Elek looked down to peer into Lily's eyes. They were half-hooded with a mix of exhaustion and desire. The look stirred his loins. Her words kicked him in the gut.

"No," he said. "I will never leave you again. If I fly away, I'll take you with me."

She smiled at that. "So we're doing this?"

"Doing what?"

"Claiming each other?"

Elek's wings exploded from his back. They enfolded around her, shutting out all of the moon's light. His claws dug deeper into her skin, somehow managing not to prick her flesh and draw blood.

Lily didn't startle at the display. She pressed her body more firmly against his, her soft flesh meeting his hard planes.

She gave Elek a shove, urging him onto his back. His wings unfurled and spread out, spanning the room to grant her wish. Once she was seemingly free of her captivity, Lily mounted him.

Her slight weight on his hips felt as though Elek were grounding himself into the firm earth. In all of his years of meditation, he'd never known this level of peace and belonging.

"I claim you, Elek. I claim you as my own."

She bent her head to his neck. She pressed her lips there, causing both man and beast to shiver. Then she bit down, hard enough to break the skin.

"Ouch." He laughed.

"You're mine," she said, licking the trickle of blood from her teeth. There was a ferociousness in her gaze.

"I am," he agreed.

That got a grin out of her. His mate reached down and freed his erection. Both man and beast submitted to her will. It had never felt so good to feel helpless.

"I'll be gentle," she said.

"Don't bother."

With her body over his, Lily thrust downward and Elek roared. He had been in fear of losing control again for more than half his life. He had never imagined such pleasure could be had in surrender. Both man and beast were in agreement. They were a slave to this woman.

"I want you," she said as she rocked. "I want only you. I want all of you."

Elek gave his mate what she wanted; all of him. Man and beast. His body and spirit. His breath and his soul.

They rocked until they reached their release.

Then Elek flipped Lily over. He grabbed the belt buckle from the nightstand, the one that Lily had gifted him in hopes he'd find The Glow.

Binding his mate's hands and latching them onto the headboard so that she was immobile, Elek gave and gave to her until her body reached the upper level. As they came in a simultaneous release, their minds, bodies and souls were one.

# CHAPTER TWENTY

he front lawn was awash in neon colors. Polyester fabrics stretched over a sea of eight-pack abs that rolled and rippled in time to the music. Denim cupped firm asses which shimmied and thrusted to the beat.

Konan had his wolf brothers clustered to one side. The wolves were decked out in Adidas track suits, while on their feet were Puma Clydes. The caps they wore proclaimed shifter wolves were all a part of the Dynamic Wolverines Crew.

Meanwhile, the Beastie Bears sported Puma track suits with Adidas Gazelles on their feet. Turin's thick thighs were up in the air as he practiced his head spins on flattened cardboard boxes laid out on the grass. The bear bounded to his feet and slapped palms with each of his five brothers.

Between the wolves and bears were the lions, or rather the Roar Steady Crew. Izem and Leander were decked out in pink-and-orange t-shirts and cut-off jeans with graffiti sprayed across the fabric. Surprisingly, the pastel neon colors worked for their golden skin tones. The lions' big bodies performed robotic-like movements, popping and locking to the rhythm of the music playing from the boom box.

It would have been an amazing breakdance battle. Too bad it was no longer needed. Maybe the shifters would still perform in celebration of Lily's news? Though she doubted there would be any enthusiasm over what she had to say to the men.

Lily squeezed Elek's hand. His claws were still out, and so the edge of his nail dug into her skin. The sting reassured Lily more than his words ever could. Which was a good thing, since Elek hadn't used his vocal chords since they'd left her bedroom.

When Ilia and Rose had seen the two coming out of Lily's bedroom together, Elek's response to his brother asking if he'd gotten any sleep was a deep-throated growl. Same when Kimber asked if he needed to cancel the mating-games play-date and send all their friends home. Lily had taken on the response to that question, and now they were here on the lawn.

"Everything's ready, Lily," said Cardi with her clipboard in her hand. "The lions are up first, performing to Kurtis Blow's *The Breaks.* Then the wolves are gonna perform to Tone Loc's *Wild Thing.* The bears have *Planet Rock,* which is my personal favorite and—"

"Cardi." Kimber came to stand beside his mate, his brow raised as he looked out at the competing shifters dressed like they were castoffs from *Breaking Two: Electric Boogaloo.* "The games are over."

"What? No, you said we could do this. Wait! I don't even need your permission. It's what Lily wants."

Kimber cocked his head towards Lily. Lily still held Elek's hand, but Elek had moved behind her. His other arm was wrapped loosely around her midsection. Lily knew that if she were to try to move away, she'd get nowhere fast. Luckily, she didn't mind being caged in by Elek. She had no plans to run anywhere.

"It looks like Lily has exactly what she wants," said Kimber.

Cardi opened her mouth to protest some more. As she took the two of them in, recognition dawned on her pretty face. Her eyes didn't light up like Chryssie's and Poppy's and Rose's had. Cardi let out a sulky pout.

"Fine," she sighed. And then, "Man, this was going to be epic. When are we going to get them to do another dance battle?"

Kimber chuckled, tucking his mate into his side. He whispered something in her ear that put the light back in her eyes. It also put a saucy smile on her lips.

Around them, the others of the weyr nodded their approval. No one, not the dragons or the women, seemed surprised. Though the women were definitely put out that their fun was over.

Rose winked at her sister, then wiped a tear from the corner of her eyes. Lily blinked tears of her own away. This was the biggest job she and her sister had ever gone for, and they'd landed it. They'd both gotten their happily ever after. It was bigger than walking Paris Fashion Week or getting the cover of *Sports Illustrated.* This gig lasted forever and paid better. Because you couldn't put a price on happiness.

Lily gave Elek a nudge. She knew he wouldn't let her go up on the stage by herself. Not with the dragon so close to the surface. In fact, she wasn't sure which was in control.

Not that it mattered. She loved them both. She loved them separate, as much as she loved them as a whole.

The dancing stopped when she came to stand before her throne on the stage. All of the males looked up at her. No, they looked past her at the hold Elek had on her.

Lily knew her statement would likely be more powerful if she stood on her own and made this speech. But she wasn't alone anymore. She never would need to be, and so she held her mate's hand as she spoke into the microphone.

"I want to thank you all for coming today," she began. "I want to thank you for participating in these mating games. It's meant a lot to me that you would put yourselves out there the way you have."

Down on the grassy knoll, Leander scratched at his neon-pink headband, shoving the fabric further back on his head to push his blond locks out of his eyes.

"It's given me a boost of confidence and made me feel worthy," Lily continued. She glanced over her shoulder at Elek, seeking his strength before continuing. "I want you all to know that I've made my choice and—"

"Was this a game?" Konan barked up at her. "Were you doing this to make us all look like fools?"

A low growl hummed through in Lily's ear. Somehow she knew that no one else but her could hear it. The growl was only telepathically shared with her. Elek didn't tighten his hold on her. It was Lily who tightened her hold on him.

"When I came here, I didn't want a mate. Men weren't kind to me back in the other world. They've always wanted something from me, and I didn't always want to give it."

"So you choose the man who rejected you?" said Konan. "If that isn't some fucked-up psychology."

"It's actually a very common trait in modern women," said Leander. "It's why the use of the safe word has been normalized in today's society. That way, partners can explore their sexuality and desires without shame over their proclivities."

"I didn't reject her," Elek said quietly. "I couldn't accept the love she offered me because I was too busy rejecting myself. Now that I've accepted myself, I can accept her."

"Wow, that's deep, man." Leander pounded his chest. "Mad respect."

"Fuck this," said Konan. "We tried the new rules. I'm going back to old rules. We fight for the woman."

"There will be no fighting," said Kimber. "Lily has made her choice."

The wolf ignored this. Konan took a step forward, unzipping the top of his Adidas track suit to reveal his bare chest. Konan's chest only remained bare for a split second before dark tufts of hair sprung forth to cover his pecs. Incisors glinted in the noonday sun as his wolf came out to play.

Lily's only thought was to hold on to Elek. It was Elek who let go of her.

In a flash, his flesh burst into a flame of orange scales. His claws glinted in the sunlight. Black wings exploded from his back as he raced towards the wolf.

All while Lily held onto him. Her hold on the man she loved was no match for the dragon's strength. She lost her grip on his forearm as he leaped from the stage.

She felt herself airborne, and falling in the same heartbeat. A bruising pain blossomed at the back of her head. Then everything went black.

# CHAPTER TWENTY-ONE

*E*lek's fist had been coiled to strike, his body ready to do maximum damage. Both man and dragon were of one accord on that. The wolf dared to aggress towards Lily, his Lily. It would be the last aggression the overgrown dog would ever make.

Elek would show no mercy.

He allowed the dragon to explode from his body. The change came on so swiftly that the transformation was audible. His spine cracked and reformed with plates as tough as steel. His bared teeth sharpened with an audible *ping* as fangs replaced his incisors. His wings burst from his back, fully extending and causing a gust of wind that lifted everyone's hair a few inches off their shoulders.

Everyone's except Cardi's, whose hair held so much hairspray that it barely moved a millimeter in light of Elek's display.

Man and beast leaped into the air. They were of one mind of what needed to be done. That was, to rip the wolf apart.

A blast of pain detonated at the back of Elek's head. He shook his head, confused. There had been no attacker at his rear. Konan advanced in front of him, although the wolf's offensive strides now slowed. His features morphed from determined destruction to wide-eyed worry.

And still the pain persisted at the back of Elek's head. His beast roared at the pain as it spread down his neck, down his spine and into his heart. What witchcraft was this?

When Elek felt the pain ripping at his soul, he knew…

He turned to confront his worst nightmare. Lily lay sprawled on the ground behind him. Her hair fanned out around her head like she was an angel. A steady stream of blood flowed from the back of her head and into the hungry earth.

Someone had hurt her? How had this happened? He'd stood in front of her. He and his beast had come together to protect her.

Then Elek remembered another time he and his beast had come together to protect a woman. He had accidentally struck his mother as he'd faced off against his father, who'd wanted to do the frail woman more damage by putting more whelps inside of her womb. Elek's wing had struck his mother, turning her into the silent creature she was now.

His wings had struck again.

"Get her inside," someone called.

Elek didn't know who. He stood frozen, caught in a paralysis of his own making, as he stared in horror at the woman he loved. The woman he craved. The woman he could not live this life without.

Her breaths were slow and shaky. Her heartbeat was thready. Was he losing her? He couldn't lose her.

She was there. She just needed to wake up. He knew how to wake her up. He needed to touch her.

Ilia moved forward, his arms open towards Lily's body. That brought Elek into motion. He blocked his brother, shoving him out of the way with a meaty claw.

Elek scooped Lily into his arms. Her head lolled back as he brought her to his chest. Red blood trickled down onto his amber scales. She did not open her eyes.

"Elek, we need to get her inside."

Perhaps it was his scales that weren't doing the job. When he'd held her in the past to chase away the witch on her back, it was always flesh to flesh. The dragon eagerly gave over control. Elek cradled Lily closer to his bare chest, wrapping his forearms more tightly around her.

Still, she did not wake.

"Elek, let us help her."

She was his mate. *He* was meant to help her. Maybe he needed to remove her clothing? That would bring more skin in contact with his.

Or perhaps a kiss? That was skin to skin. She had breathed life into him with their first kiss. Surely that would bring her back to him.

Elek pressed his mouth to hers. He felt the warmth leaving her in real time. She did not respond to him. She did not wake. Her lips grew colder and colder, no matter how hard he pressed his lips to hers.

"Elek, please."

That plea came from Rose. There was desperation in Rose's voice. The same growing desperation in Elek.

Elek rose with Lily in his arms. He did not let her go. He followed where his brothers guided him. He placed Lily on the mattress they told him to. He did not let her go as Corun tended to her wound.

Lily did not open her eyes. Color did not return to her cheeks. She did not reach out to him through the bond they shared.

She was silent.

He was losing her. She was leaving him.

Inside, the dragon roared. The agony was too great.

Elek wanted to blame the beast, but they'd done this together. They'd made the decision to attack. They'd acted as one when they'd struck out.

"She's going to be okay." Rose's words were wobbled. They sounded part question, part plea.

Elek couldn't look into her eyes. He couldn't look at anyone. He'd believed his beast was a menace for a long time. Now he knew for certain it wasn't just the beast. It was the both of them. It was all of him.

Lily lay on the bed. Eyes closed. Silent. Unreachable.

One by one, Elek uncurled his fingers from Lily's hand. Once she was free of him, he rose and left the room. On heavy feet, Elek climbed the stairs to his mother's room.

Mom sat slumped in her bed. Her vacant gaze was on the television set that showed a blank screen. Elek went to her, arranging the pillows so that she was upright and comfortable. Next he turned on an old sitcom about the perfect family, complete with a laugh track every time the precocious kids got caught in shenanigans, along with string music when the parents sat them down to share the lesson of the week.

With his mother settled in a fantasy world that would run for at least the rest of the night, Elek kissed her on the cheek. Then he climbed onto the balcony and jumped.

# CHAPTER TWENTY-TWO

This wasn't a dream. She was awake. And yet, Lily still couldn't move.

She didn't feel the normal crawlies on her skin. She felt nothing. Not cold or warmth. Not pressure of any kind. What was this?

She heard her sister talking to her. She heard the others talking about her. What she couldn't hear, what she couldn't sense in the room where she was, was Elek.

Where was her mate? Why wasn't he with her? He promised he'd never fly away again. Yet, she knew he wasn't here.

Not the man. Not the dragon. Some part of her knew he'd flown away. Because if Elek was here, she wouldn't be trapped in her mind. His touch could bring her back.

More than anything, Lily wanted to be brought back. She did not want to stay here in this dark, cold place. Not when Elek was warm sunshine.

Why had he left her in the dark?

He wouldn't have done it if he could help it. Of that much, Lily was certain. There had to be something wrong. There had to be something keeping him from her.

Lily wracked her brain, going over the last few moments before everything had gone black. All she could remember was pain. Pain and fear. She hadn't been afraid of Elek. He never would have brought her pain.

In her mind's eye, she saw a light. A bright, shining light. Lily backed away from the light.

Everyone knew what a bright light meant. It meant this couldn't be a dream. It meant she was—

A hand landed on Lily's shoulder. She yelped as she jumped back. She turned, expecting to find a hooded figure with hands of bones. Instead, she saw....

"Mom?"

Miyaoaxochitl stood there, eyes wide open,

staring up at Lily. Then she did something Lily had never seen her do. She blinked.

Mom's brown cheeks were vibrant in the shining light. Her hazel eyes were alive, with golden flecks at their centers. The gray was gone from her hair, leaving it a dark raven that fell in long waves down her back. The older woman—whom Lily had only ever seen slumped in a bed—looked fresh-faced and young, ready to take on the world.

"You are a pretty one, aren't you," said Mom. "I couldn't see that in the other world."

The other world? Which meant, "Are we dead?"

Mom inhaled deeply. Her eyes looked up at the darkness surrounding them above. Her gaze turned to the bright light behind them. She let out a long, throaty exhale that sounded like relief.

"Not quite," was her response.

A shudder ran down Lily's spine. Despite the light, it was cold here, so cold. A voice whispered in her head that if she drew closer to the light, she would get warm. Her feet moved towards it without a conscious decision.

"No, *une*. That is not for you."

Mom grasped Lily by both her shoulders and tugged her back against her chest. Unlike their surroundings, Mom was warm. Even better, she smelled of Elek's cooking. The feel of Mom, and the smell of her, warred with Lily's need to get closer to the heat of the light.

"What is that?" Lily asked, her gaze focused on the light.

Mom turned Lily around, putting her back to the light and moving her farther away from its source. "I need you to go and find my son."

"Elek's here?"

"Not now. But if you do not hurry, he will be coming here."

Lily turned her head, looking over her shoulder to seek the light. "Is this a bad place?"

"No, *une*. It is a good place."

Mom placed her fingers under Lily's chin and turned her head away from the light. In the opposite direction of the white glow, another light shone. This one was a rainbow of infinite shades. The color that shone the brightest was the orange of amber.

"Go and find my son, *une*. Save him from the darkness."

Lily took a step towards the colorful light. "Aren't you coming with me?"

But when Lily turned around, Mom was gone.

# CHAPTER TWENTY-THREE

Once again, Elek found himself crashing through the woods. But this time, he wasn't battling his inner dragon. Both man and beast were in control. Both of the same mind.

They flew over the grounds and beyond the forest. The flight was silent. Not a leaf at the top of any tree, not a bird's nest, not any living thing was disturbed on this aerial journey. Elek wanted to alert no one to his final destination.

Smoke curled up from the chimney of God's Teet. Down below, he saw Mari leaned against the back door, a nearly empty bottle of drink grasped in her hand. She tilted her head back and downed the last drop, swaying a bit.

Even from this distance, Elek couldn't miss the

hopelessness in her eyes. He knew that if the two of them stood face to face, she would see the same reflected in his eyes. Both of them had forever lost the ones they loved.

Mari contented herself with drink. Elek didn't care to down any spirits. He preferred to become one.

He came in for a landing as the air grew thin. His feet hit the ground, and he still had trouble breathing. He had trouble walking forward. His body insisted on backpedaling. It took the efforts of both man and dragon to propel himself to the boundary of the Veil.

Each step was like daggers in his feet. Each breath burned his lungs, dousing the fire within. Dragons were not meant to cross the veil between the two worlds. The Goddess had not designed Her shifters to live in the world beyond, which is exactly why Elek was crossing there.

That's where his Lily would be. Not back in the human world. She had gone to the World After, the world of the spirits. This was the only way he could get there. He needed to get to her quickly. He didn't want her to be alone for too long. He'd promised.

Another step brought him just over the edge. Everything in his body protested. Elek felt like he was drowning, but instead of being submerged in water, he was floating in a vacuum. Fire couldn't exist in a vacuum.

Yet, up ahead, Elek saw a faint glow. It moved closer and closer to him, the light burned brighter than any fire he'd ever seen. It was a golden glow.

A form stepped out of the light. The hourglass shape of the form told Elek that a woman was walking toward him. It had to be her. It had to be Lily. She was the one Elek sought.

It took only a second for Elek to know that it wasn't his mate. This woman had raven-colored hair, as black as night. She was short, nearly half Lily's modelesque stature. And she was glaring at him with her hands on round hips as though she were about to scold him for being a naughty child.

"You are grounded."

"Mom?"

"Exactly what do you think you're doing with your life? This is not how I raised you to behave."

The lack of air had gone to Elek's head. He dropped to his knees and hugged his mom around the middle. When her arms cradled his head, Elek could do nothing but bury his face in her chest.

There was no heartbeat there. Her chest didn't rise and fall with breath. He didn't care about that.

For more years than he wanted to count, all Elek had ached for was his mother's touch. To hear the sound of her voice. Even if it was to scold.

"I should have left a long time ago," Mom said as she smoothed out his hair. "But someone had to stay and watch over you."

"You were watching over me?"

"Of course, I was. Now you have a good woman to look after you and I can finally go and rest."

Mom gave Elek a tug and urged him to his feet. Elek was slow to rise. The last memory he had of his mother with fire in her eyes was when he was still small and he'd had to look up at her. His dragon had never been small, which was why it had caused her the damage.

Mom grabbed at Elek's chin. She peered into his eyes, staring hard. Elek knew what she wanted. She wanted to speak to his dragon.

Amber flashed in Elek's eyes, but the dragon had trouble holding his mother's gaze. Once again, Mom lifted her son's chin.

"You protected me from that monster. I would have been dead long ago if not for you. I would not have had the chance to watch my son grow into a man I'm proud of."

Tears would have spilled from Elek's eyes. But

the fire of the glow from within consumed each and every one before they could form. Elek wrapped his arms around his mother and squeezed. Miyaoaxochitl squeezed her son with a strength no one would've believed of the small woman.

"I sent Lily after you. She should be here now. Go, go and make me some beautiful grand babies I can watch over from the world beyond."

Mom stepped back towards the light. Elek held her hand for as long as he could. Her smiling eyes full of light was the last thing he saw of his mother.

Elek blinked, and she was gone. What was left was darkness. The dark was so absolute that he couldn't tell which way to go to get back to his world.

Arms came around him. The arms felt familiar, and so he didn't resist when they pulled. Instinctively, Elek knew to allow those arms to guide him back home.

A second later and his lungs filled with fresh air. His eyes opened to see the dark of night lit by a starry sky. He turned and saw that he was surrounded by everyone in his family; each of his brothers, and the women who they'd pledged their lives to. Elek's gaze settled on the bright flame holding onto him. He wrapped his arms around Lily, breathing in the warmth of her glow.

"You flew away again," she said.

"I was flying after you."

Lily's gaze flicked to the disturbance in the air that veiled this world from her old world. She knew what it meant if she stepped across that line, so she knew what it meant if he did the same. She squeezed him tighter and her nails dug into his back.

"What happened wasn't your fault," she said.

"It was. But Mom reminded me that I was raised to be better."

"You saw her, too?" Lily looked again to the shifting light of the Veil.

"She grounded me."

Lily quirked a brow at that. All worry vanished from her features. "Does that mean you have to stay in your bedroom?"

For the first time today, Elek's lips stretched into a grin. The dragon peered out at his mate with a glowing fire of desire.

"I'll keep you company." Lily pressed a kiss to his lips. She ended the kiss with a bite to his lower lip, hard enough to draw blood. "I'm going to stay with you forever."

Elek licked his lips. Then he scooped his mate

into his arms. At his back, the dragon spread his wings. His wings carried him and his mate up high in the sky. Away from the light of the Veil. Away from the glow of the moon. Neither had to search for anything outside of themselves when the love they shared blazed so bright.

Are you ready for the final story of this world?
I suspect you know the who the last remaining love story features.
But wait until you see how Rhoyl's and Mari's love story began
in *The Dragon's Forbidden Sacrifice,*
the sixth and final book of The Last Dragons series!

Lover of fairytales, folklore, and mythology, Ines Johnson spends her days reimagining the stories of old in a modern world. She writes books where damsels cause the distress, princesses wield swords, and moms save the world.

You can sign up for her mailing list and receive alerts and free reads at https://ineswrites.com/ReaderGroup.

**The Last Dragons**

The Dragon's Reluctant Sacrifice

The Dragon's Ambivalent Sacrifice

The Dragon's Willing Sacrifice

The Dragon's Rebellious Sacrifice

The Dragon's Compliant Sacrifice

The Dragon's Forbidden Sacrifice